Trapped by the unexpected .

Chapter 1

Abbey

I was glad it was finally Friday, and that meant a break from the bougie ass, rich kids. Who knew that name brand clothing could make someone an asshole? Friday was my day to run out of school, and not worry about the headaches they caused daily. It was my senior year at Fisher Prep, and I am three weeks away from being eighteen, and I was ready to move to Florida for college. My dad stayed on my ass about keeping my grades up, and I did not disappoint him. His determination for me to graduate with honors was not as big as my determination to move and be in my own spot. I was over his ass.

My best friends since fourth grade, Farrah and Bailey would hopefully be by my side when the time to move came. They were party animals though, and I did not know where that would lead us. When I was trying to finish my homework, they were all over the place having fun.
While they did them, I was sitting outside of the school, working on my homework. I was completely frustrated that I was stuck on question two. I wanted to pull all my curls out, I stopped stressing for a moment, and looked over the work. Just as I was about to get my answer prepared, my crazy ass best friends waited up, breaking my train of thought as they always did anyway.

"Girl I heard it's this party tonight!!", Farrah said smiling

"Where at?", I asked

"On the Southside ", she said blowing a kiss at me

"Trying to go?", Bailey asked

"Yes bitch let's turn the fuck up," I said laughing putting my books away

Little did they know this party was an escape for me and something I really needed. Once I was done I made my way home to get ready, and the closer I got the more I felt uneasy. I prayed my father was not home, so I would not have to deal with what was to come. I made it there after a fifthteen minute walk and I noticed right away my father's car was not in the driveway, so I knew he was not home.

I walked in shutting the door behind me as my body got tense. I knew my mother but did not because I was only seven years old when she left. I would not dare question my father about it again, after the beating I got before. I made it to my room in a hurry to take a shower and get dressed, before my father made it home, after my thirty-minute shower I walked back in my room with my towel around me looking for something to wear.

"Shit what the fuck!! I don't have shit to wear to this dam party"

I threw my clothes around searching for anything when I came across, my black leggings and yellow spaghetti string top with my jewelry. I pulled out my yellow Converse before letting my hair down. I sprayed my honey of river oil on and looked at myself one last time before walking out. I met up with my girls and Farrah started telling us the latest news

.

"Aaron is going to be at the party!!" Farrah said.

"Bitch your lying." I spoke in one breath.

Our childhood best friend was in town and I hoped it would be like old times. We have not seen Aaron in like five years since our dads moved us away claiming he was bad company and we were not doing well in school. We arrived thirty minutes later, and the music was loud, people were all over the yard, so we joined the party. This party was live, and they had food, and drinks with servers going around. This lady came up to us giving us a drink and the perfume she was wearing reminded me of my mother. I do not remember her face, but I could remember that smell from miles away. I wished for years that she would come for me but wishes just would not come true I believed; My thoughts were broken when this group of boys walked past me talking and one of their hands touched my butt, it ticked me off, so I turned around to mean mugging them all.

"What did you say? ", I asked with my hands on my hip

"Chill out ma!! My bad didn't mean no harm ", he said smiling

"Next time watch it, or you'll get hurt ", I said again

"Abbey is that you?", the other asked coming into the light

"Aaron?", I questioned

Aaron gave each of us a hug, and Bailey almost fainted which made me crack up. He was like a brother to Farrah and I; , whereas Bailey and he had crushes on each other. I wish Aaron and Bailey would just kiss already and get together because this has been going on for years. My thoughts were broken when Aaron began trying to speak over all the music.

"yawl hanging with us tonight" Aaron asked us

"I guess. I don't really hang with these clowns though" I said rolling my eyes

"Oh, really so you know them already?" he asked me

"They don't really hang with girls like us at school because we are thick and all" Bailey said

"Man, they are not the type of people to hang out with but Farrah on the other hand can get it" Aden said

"Look at them man, they don't know shit about fun why are you even talking to them anyway? Shit I don't get why she even hang with them" Faheem said shaking his head

"watch it Faheem I grew up with them and your ass don't either so shut the hell up. I bet yawl assess never gave them a chance "Aaron said

"You are damn right their pops the police" Aden said again

"What the fuck do that mean nigga we use to have mad fun, we always got into some type of trouble" Aaron said laughing

"Chill big bro dam our bad" Aden said again with his hands up

"Bro?" Bailey asked

"Well sorry I haven't mentioned that years ago but Faheem and Aden my brothers in my pops side" Aaron said in surrender

"Wow Aaron just wow" Farrah said shaking her head

"let's go outside to smoke this blunt" Aaron said

"Let's go" I said walking off

We all made our way through the party going outside to smoke, this house was big as hell and nice, It was like a mini mansion. It had the pool and Jacuzzi in the backyard then there was still room to party out there. Then there was the inside of the house. It was painted a nice red and white coloring with painting hanging almost everywhere.

I wonder who parents own this house because this shit was nice compared to what I'm used to, we sat outside smoking and talking for a while. I always have thought Aden was handsome he was about 5'9 with light brown eyes he had box braids, and was tattooed all over almost, He was very built, and it showed through his shirt, he was cool and collective but that's just not what I'm looking for right now plus he was an asshole. We got to know each other more and it felt kind of good because even though he said I was not his type I always had a crush on him. I could tell he had never been with a big girl before, but he would not know until he gave it a try. Once we were done smoking, we went back inside grabbing some drinks and my song came on, so I began dancing.

Kranium nobody has to know was my shit, and as I moved my hips from side to side popping my booty, everyone watched amazed. Dancing took my mind off everything that was going on at home, Farrah and Bailey joined in, Bailey and I big behinds were killing it. Aden pulled me to the side asking if he could speak with me in private and I agreed to follow him. We walked into this master bedroom, I walked in looking around the room noticing Aden's name going across the room, so my guess was this was their house, we sat down on the bed talking and I learned a lot about him so I thought.

"Dam Abbey you can dance that good" Aden asked smiling

"I guess you could say that" I said laughing

"What if I kissed you?" he flirted with me

"What if I smacked you?" I questioned

"Let me see that booty that big old booty" he flirted more singing

"I have no clue what made him want to talk to me suddenly, but I was enjoying the company for now. As we sat and talked he tried to touch on me and it made me feel crazy, so I smacked his hands away. I jumped up running out the door, I made it to the hall looking around before I ran down the steps fast. Leaving the house, I made my way home, my head was spinning, and I just wanted to lay down, because honestly, I was tired and just fed up. Once I made it home, I unlocked the door going straight in heading to my room. I am walking in my room, closing the door behind me.

I sat on the bed, when I heard footsteps by my door, my father's voice echoed out through the house making me jump damn near off my bed.

"Abbey is that you?", my father deep voice sounded out

"Umm yes dad ", I said quickly

"Good I need you so get in here ", he said aging

I walked down the hall to the game room to see my father was getting drunk as usual, and I knew what that meant. My father went on and on about how beautiful my eyes were, and my ass he said was even fatter than my mother's, it made me feel nasty and I wanted to be out before he tried anything crazy. He tried to touch me for the first time like he wanted to fuck me or something, so I smacked his hand away,

He smacked me across my face, and I hit the floor hard I couldn't move and there wasn't shit I could do but cry. My father continued to hit me until he got tired, and I just knew I would have to cover up all these bruises. There was no way his big ass should be hitting me. My father was short but muscular. He had big brown eyes, and black hair. He had this cut on his right cheek and was very spiteful. I really wanted my father locked away or dead because honestly, I couldn't take the beating any more and the way he looked at me made me sick.

How could you even think straight after getting a couple marbles lost up there, but even then, I hid how abusive my dad was, this was something I never wanted to share but needed to get out of it fast. I really wish my mother were around, or someone to help for that matter. I sat in my room rubbing my hands over the bruises and with every touch I flinched from the pain. I laid back on my bed thinking of why my father was the way he is, or why he treats me the way he does, the pain was unbearable, and I left like my life was going to end most times. My father always went on and on about how he did not want no daughters, just sons but my mother would not get rid of me, so he got rid of her. Deep down inside I knew she was still alive and wished she could come save me from this hell hole. I got up going to my bathroom, I walked in and stood in front of the mirror looking at myself. I hate myself right now and hated my father even more, hearing him call me a fat Bitch daily hurt like hell. My father was a police officer but a very mean one.

He used that shit to his advantage, and got away with almost everything, the problems and shit that happened at work he took out on me. My father hated me, and he just didn't know the feeling was mutual, I sat in the hot water letting my body soak while I thought of a plan, Bailey or Farrah had no clue what I dealt with from my father, because Farrah didn't have to go through it, and Bailey's father wasn't as abusive as mine. This was something I kept to myself and never told anyone, but I can look at them and see they have it better than me. They never speak about what goes on at home, but you can look at them and see it. Farrah is very needy, and Bailey is quiet. You can tell she is covering up something.

Chapter 2 Aaron

Visiting my father in jail was the worst, and I hated them damn police officers, my father was going to be locked up for 25 years, for killing three cops and a family. Leaving my brothers and I to take over his empire, our mother hated the thought of it, but I had to be there for my father. I parked my car emptying out my pockets, before going to the state prison to see my father, I walked in singing my name before going through the metal detectors. When I got in the back, they checked me, making sure I did not have anything before sending me towards the visiting area. I took a seat waiting for my pops to come out, my hands started to sweat, and I just wiped them on my pants, my father soon came out and he began talking in code about the empire.

"What up Aaron" my father said sitting down

"Nothing much pops!! What's up with you?" I asked looking at him

"Everything good man I'm hanging in there" he said shaking his head

" Man pops I'm here for you man, you know I got you" I said sitting up a little

How the family doing?" he asked me

"They good pops I have it under control" I spoke wisely

"Aden and Faheem visited me a couple days ago" he spoke looking around

"Yea what happened?" I questioned

"Man watch them Kid there up to something" he spoke firmly.

After we talked a while longer, I headed out with my father's words ringing through my head, they never told me that they visited pops and Aden ass always acting weird. Faheem was the quieter one, but you know what they say about those kinds of people right? I jumped in my truck speeding off not wanting to be near there any longer than I had to, my phone light was blinking like crazy, so I decided to check it when I got to the red light. When I reached the light, I looked at my phone seeing I had a lot of damn calls and texts from the trap house. I shook my head looking up, noticing the light turned green, and the people behind me beeping their horns at me, I pulled off flicking everyone behind me off. I heard them cursing at me, but if they know what is good for them, they will chill the fuck out.

"What the fuck!!! If it's not one thing it's another"

I pulled up to the trap house pissed as hell, getting out I saw everyone standing outside, I walked up going straight in with everyone following behind me, once I reached the basement I noticed drugs and money was missing. The place was fucked up and I knew for sure this was an inside job. Whoever tried to play me will deal with the consequences, I pulled out my phone calling my brothers only to get the voicemail, and my father's words went through my head again. I called a couple more times and Faheem answered the phone this time, I began snapping out on him not giving him time to even say hello.

"Faheem what the fuck man!!! I go see pops and my shit get robbed where the fuck where you and Aden?" I asked pissed off

"Wait what slow down bro, Aden was there watching the trap while I handled my business at the clinic" he spoke quickly

"The clinic what the fuck!! Where is Aden right now" I asked looking around

"He stopped picking the phone for me Aaron I have no clue" Faheem spoke

I hung up the phone on him because they were always together, or knew where the other one was at. I feel like I am getting set up by my own brothers, but I am way smarter than that. Trust comes a long way and I was snatching that shit back from everyone until they earned it. I made everyone go upstairs and sit down, because someone was going to spill what the fuck happened, I was just like my father in many ways, but if I fucked this up, I would get fucked up. Which was something I did not want to deal with, my uncle and pops ran this shit for years, and would fuck me up if I fucked up everything they worked for. Once I was upstairs, I see everyone sitting, so I began talking looking at their faces, seeing they was scared, but I did not give a fuck at all.

"Who was here with Aden and Where the fuck he at?" I asked looking at every one of them

"Man, Aden was here with Jon ass, I'm not scared of Aden like these nigga's" Clever said shaking his head
"What do you mean?" I questioned him

"While you're not around Aden goes on and on, about how he should be in charge, He got almost every nigga in this bitch scared" Ray said looking around

I didn't even say anything else because I knew Aden hated the fact our father put me in charge. Aden was a hot head and did not really care about shit, he was good for getting himself locked up or into trouble. I walked around looking at everyone looking at me and I knew these niggas was not loyal to me at all but Clever and Ray are different. As I got closer to Jon, I picked him up out of his seat, from around his neck as his feet dangled around, he complained about how he could not breathe. Which I could care fucking less, He began talking fast so I let him drop to the ground hard as hell.

"ADEN HAS THIS PLAN TO TAKE YOUR SPOT ON THE EMPIRE, HE SAID YOU TO PUSSY FOR THE EMPIRE, AND HE WILL PAY ME MORE THAN WHAT YOU DO. ONLY IF I HELPED, MY FAMILY NEEDS THE MONEY, SO DIDN'T THINK TWICE ABOUT IT." Jon spoke really fast

Without another word I pulled out my gun sending three shots to his body, one to the head and two to the chest, I did not play about my money or non-loyal mother fuckers. He got paid well because I knew his problems at home, and he stabbed me in the back. Aden had always been the problem with his wild ass, and now he just took it way too far. If my father found out about this shit which I am sure he would, all hell is going to break loose. I walked out calling Aden again only to get no answer, I jumped in my car heading towards my mother house. I usually check on my mother every day, but shit been crazy, so I really have not had the chance too. Faheem and Aden were a couple of months apart, Aden was wilder than Faheem and me, put together he was a hot ass mess you could not tell him nothing. My mother took them in and raised them as her own when their mother ran off. I could not wait to get my hands on him, because I am going to beat the shit out of him, like pops should have long ago. I pulled up to my mother's house, just as my phone began ringing, answering without looking it was not who I expected. The operator began talking, and I got nervous about what the hell my father was about to say. Hello, you have a collect call from Amir, to accept this call press zero, to block all calls from this, caller press one. Not wanting to hear no more, I pressed zero to accept the call, and my father wasted no time yelling.

"WHAT THE FUCK HAPPENED AARON? WHY DO I HEAR ADEN GOING AGAINST YOU, ROBBING MY PLACES? I TOLD YOU TO WATCH HIS ASS, DO YOU WANT TO SEE WHAT I CAN DO FROM THIS DAMN PLACE?"

"Pops calm down, I'm handling it, I have everything under control, trust me" I spoke carefully

"Don't fuck with me Aaron, I trust you" He said more calmer

Before I could say anything else, he hung up the phone, I sat out there for a while longer. I need to get my mind right, and fast because Aden was fucking up. My father's words from the visit popped back up in my head, I got what he meant when he said watch them now, I could not believe Aden was doing this shit but then who am I kidding. I did not want shit to do with this empire, and told my father constantly that this was not the life I wanted for myself. Since Aden or Faheem did not want to take charge I was forced to, now his ass does not like my rules so now he wants to be in charge. My father did not really trust Aden, but he would have given him the empire since he was so damn heartless. My father also knew that Aden would have fucked up, the money on them hoes he mess with, I finally got out the car going inside the house. I walked into my mother's house to cook food, shit smelled good, she was cooking Mac and cheese with some fried chicken and corn bread.

"Aaron is that you" my mother yelled

"How did you know mom?" I questioned her

"Boy I'm your mother, that's how, now get in here and sit down." She said again

I made my way to the kitchen to see my mother cooking it up, Faheem was sitting at the table with his head looking down into his books. Faheem was not a street nigga at all, but the boy had hands. I walked over to take a seat next to him and we began talking. Mom left the kitchen for a while because they were calling out the numbers to the lottery.

"What's been up Lil dude" I said smirking

"Stop calling me that, and nothing much your brother tripping" he said looking back down at his books

"Why what happens" I asked him

"He want to take you out and I'm just not with it, I honestly don't give a fuck about that dam empire" he said a little upset and mad

"Look Heem you know I don't give a fuck about it either but remember daddy don't trust him, he will just use all the money on them hoes. I want out of this just as much as you do baby bro trust me" I said shaking my head

"Aaron, I know this wasn't your life and it's why you left before but bro I need you, I can't count on Aden unless I'm helping him with some fuck shit"

Just then mom walked back in, and I acted like I was helping him with his homework. She smiled at us, and went back to cooking. I got up and went into the living room to turn on the game. Faheem's words kept playing in my head, and I knew he did not have shit to do with Aden, but why go against me now was my question for Aden. The game came back on, and I began watching it. I need to get me and Faheem out of this for good. One thing for sure and one thing for certain, is that pops is going to be pissed, and I prayed no one will have to get hurt in the process.

Chapter 3
Bailey

I haven't spoken to Abbey since the party, and I wondered if she was ok because her father was worse than mine most times. As I finished getting dressed for school I could hear my father coming through the front door, my heart rate sped up as I slipped my shoes on. A knock was on my room door soon, as my hand touched it, I jumped back out of fear. When the door flew open my father walked in, and I just knew I was not making it to school on time, each time I backed up he came closer to me. My father had this light natural skin with heavy sunken brown eyes, he had well-kept black hair with a thin chinstrap. When he raised his hand at me, I flinched, and he laughed, looking back up at him a smack, went across my face hard and I fell on my bed. He was an average height, with thin arms and legs but these shits hurt badly.

"Bitch I know you was at that party, with Abbey and Farrah, the other night" he spoke loudly

"Dad why did you hit me" I asked with tears rolling down my face

"Bitch i'll hit you every time I get ready!! You know that's why your mother, not here anymore she asked too many damn question, instead of doing what I asked" he said spitting at me

"There was no point in, killing her dad she was already sick" I cried a *little more*

"If she would have just minded her business and let me do what I want to you then she would still be here. But lucky me because she gone, and I can do what I please, you have no help" he laughed walking out

I just stood there a little while longer because I was scared, and he was right I had no help, the lust I saw in his eyes was the same look Abbey father gave her daily. I pulled out my phone calling Abbey back to back and got no answer, calling Farrah she picked up.

"What up bitch" she semi yelled through the phone

"Have you spoken to Abbey?" I asked her

"No, I haven't, I'm quite sure the bitch OK, why yawl always acting like yawl father's so bad. I mean I'll be glad to have my father as a cop, instead of a damn professor." She said mad

"Wow Farrah did you just really say that?" I question her

"Look Bailey I need to go, I will talk to yawl later, I need yawl later" she said hanging up

Farrah was really starting to irk my nerves, she thought just because our fathers was, cops that we should be happy. There was not shit good about this, she had it good, her parents let her do whatever; As long her grades were good. Abbey and I tried to go to the cops plenty of times, but they only called our fathers saying we are making up false statements about them which only made me believe that they ass feared them also. I really did not know what our father had them at the station thinking, but I knew for sure they had everyone fooled. I went to the mirror that hung on my wall and looked in it to see this black and blue bruise across my face. I shook my head pulling out my makeup bag to cover up the mark, before walking out of here. When I was done, I grabbed my things, wasting no time, to get the hell out of this house. I hated my father with a passion, and I wanted him to just finally disappear. Once I made it to school after a fifteen minute walk my mind still raced, to what my father said. I walked in the school building, with all eyes on me, and I kept it pushing to my locker.

I could hear them whisper about how big I was, or how I needed to go to the gym, and I brushed it off. I made it to my class, and noticed Abbey sitting with her head towards the window. Which was something she never did unless something happened. Aden and Faheem walked into class with their hoes, and they all began talking about us. I found it funny how fast they switched up for them lame ass hoes. I sat next to Abbey, and we started our work, she looked at me and we both were covering up something our fathers did. I looked over at Faheem, and his corny ass crew, the look on his face showed that it was not him, but since he hangs with them and doesn't say a word he is just as guilty as the rest of them. I wanted to fuck one of them up, so bad but I did not want to risk getting suspended, or I will have to deal with more beatings from my father then I already have too. Soon that diploma hit my hands I am fucking shit up, with help from my best friends, for my father's health he better hopes I do not kill his ass that day too. We all went to a college far away from our families, and they did not even know it. Abbey began talking, and her voice cracked the moment, the words left her mouth.

"Bailey, why would my mother leave me with such a ruthless man like my father?" she whispered

"Boo I doubt if she just up, and left you like Mr. Ron says!!! My honest feeling is that he did something to her also" I spoke my truth on it for the first time

"Maybe your right and I over think it but how could I not when she hasn't been around since I could remember" she wiped her eyes from the tears

We finished our work just as the bell rang throughout the school, we put our books away; handing in our papers before going out the door. As we made our way down the hall people started talking about us and we kept it moving, this whole school needed Jesus and to pass some fucking classes instead of sucking each other dicks daily. Abbey rolled her eyes as her phone began to ring, her face was scrunched up and I knew for sure it was her dad. Our fathers were very malicious and would do anything out of spite and it killed us inside, people laughed when our fathers showed out, but I just could not understand what was so damn funny.

"Abbey and Bailey let's fucking go now!!!" Mr. Ron screamed out

"Why are you here daddy?" Abbey asked

"Bitch bring your big ass on" Mr. Ron said

"HA YOU BIG BITCH" Everyone laughed out

We just walked out following behind him and I knew for sure Abbey was hurt because I was. Farrah came out with a crew of people not too long after, and we headed towards the house. You could smell the liquor coming from their clothes and I knew they were drunk at 1:45 in the afternoon. My real questions were why they are not at work, my father's phone began ringing and he answered it on speaker.

"Officer Harrison the captain need yawl in the office right now" the girl voice sounded out through the phone

"What do he want now" Mr. Ron asked

"He didn't say" she said again

My father just hung up the phone, and Ron made his way to the station, to see what the caption wanted. Once we arrived my father made me get into his car and wait for him.

Ron

The captain was really pissing me off, and no one knew about me whooping Abbey ass because I put a show on for the captain. He was not going to give us that promotion, then he could kiss my black ass, there was this big drug bust and promotion he promised us. We walked in and took seats ready to hear the good news.

"So, I have good news and some bad news" he said smiling

"Give us the bad news first" I said

"Well my nephew just arrived, and he will be doing the drug bust, meaning he gets the promotion" he said

"WHAT THE FUCK DID YOU SAY?" Harrison questions him

"Now Tom we had a deal, and you fucking us over?" I asked him

"Look fellas, the good news is you could spend more time with your families!! I'll put in a couple extra bucks, for all the hard work but my hands are tied on this one" Tom said looking at us

Flipping his desk over we made our way back outside, I hated to be fucked over, and he will soon realize how much I hate it. We stood outside talking about what we were going to do, tears will be shed, and that promotion will be ours. I jumped in my car heading home *forgetting Abbey was in the car until her phone made some crazy ass sound. Abbey mom was not dead because I ran the bitch away by beating her ass, I was very Malicious, and I did not care about a damn thing. Most times I felt bad that Abbey, got caught in the crossfire but then again, I did not really give a fuck either. She was a weak bitch, and would not dare talk back to me. I knew the spiteful harmful shit I did made her hurt badly, but I did not care at all. I pulled up to the house, and we made our way in, pulling my bottle out of my pocket. I took a couple more sips. I looked up to see Abbey going inside, and I stared at her for a while before going in. Abbey had a deep set of blue eyes, like her mother with full lips, and small ears. She was a medium height, with a curvy body, and blond/black shoulder length hair which reminded so much of her mother.*

I never wanted any daughters, just sons, but since Alice did not get rid of her, she came in handy for certain shit. As Abbey grew older her body formed in ways I did not think it would, she had Alice shape. I wanted to fuck Abbey like I did, her mother and, she already got the body like her. Abbey was not my daughter, at least in my mind, she was not, she was more of a roommate to me. I was going to get her, and she did not have any help, so the bitch was out of luck. I took a couple more sips, thinking about how Tom ass fucked me over, Abbey was going to feel all my pain, even if it killed her ass. I took almost everything out on her ass just like I did her mother. Alice went down for some months behind some shit I did, and I was the cop who took her ass in, she never listened to me, so I showed her ass the true me. I was tired of people trying me, I was spiteful and did not mind, putting a bullet in someone's head. I had no regret to shit I did, and if we are being honest, I was the one who took, Aaron father to jail we had a deal and he fucked it up. I mean he killed Tom's brother, wife and kids but, he did not do exactly what I wanted him to. I was a very spiteful mother fucker that, my family did not even fuck with me. My mother warned Alice about me plenty of times but she was just too blind, by the fake love I threw her way daily.

Chapter 4
Aaron

I still haven't got my hands-on Aden yet, but I will see that ass real soon. I haven't really spoken to Abbey and Bailey since the party, I see Farrah wild ass all the time. I figured out why, everything in me hated their fathers, and I knew something was not right with them, growing up they would be looking crazy. During the summertime they wore sweatpants and long sleeve shirts, after watching how Malicious their dads were it struck something in me. How can you treat your child like that? In front of the whole school, Faheem texted me saying they were on their way out, and I waited patiently. I parked my truck, so it would not be noticed, and stood on the side of the school watching everyone come out. Once I spotted Aden, I snatched his ass up, without another thought, everyone stopped and looked while he acted tuff.

"Aaron what the fuck!!! Keep your hands off my clothes like that, you are messing up my clothes Neff" Aden said with his face scrunched up

"Aden man chill, he pissed off" Faheem butted in

"I don't give a damn, how pissed off he is, he better go somewhere" Aden said shaking his head

I never said a word, but my next move is to fuck him up, I grabbed him around the neck squeezing it, just enough for him to get; I'm not our father.

"Aden stop fucking with me OK!! Now I know you did that shit back, at the empire and you will pay for it. Mark my words Neff" I said mocking his tone of voice

I let him go and he fell to the ground catching his breath. I wasn't playing with his ass, and I will show him how serious I am. I am tired of playing this game with him, and Faheem better keep his ass in line. I walked back to my truck, jumping in and pulling off, Aden had me fucked up. For years he tried to play the big brother role, and always had us in trouble with the law, and everyone else but not this time. He talked as if shit did not mean, nothing to him, he barely went to check or see our mother unless he needed something. I was about to put, my foot down on a lot of shit, I had to go out of town for a business trip, but how could I trust Faheem to keep Aden out my Empire, and in his mother fucking lane. Once I arrived home, I pulled out my phone sending Abbey a text praying she answered.

"Hey Ab, I need yawl help with something"

"Sure, what's the word" She replied right away

"Keep an eye on my brothers!! I am going out of town, and don't trust Aden right now" I mentioned

"No worries we got you bro, oh and he looks untrustworthy" she said again

"Good look!! I could always count on yawl" I replied

I waited for a while but never got a text back from her, I got out my truck locking the doors, behind me heading inside the house. I unlocked the door going in, and made my way upstairs to pack up, so it would not be last minute, I would be gone at least two weeks and needed a close eye kept on Aden ass. I could count on Abbey, and them to be there for me though, Bailey and I finally confessed how we felt about each other, and I was glad she felt the same way. We had sex, but I wanted to make love to her, like with Slow jams playing, Wine and strawberries, with whipped cream, you know what I mean.

About three hours later, I started to pack up my truck when this lady interrupted me. Looking back I see Abbey's mom standing right before my eyes. I watched Abbey talk about her mom, all the time and now, she was here standing right before my eyes. I pulled out my phone, calling Abbey but it only went to voicemail which was wired. That girl always had her phone on, and now she is not even answering, she would be damn happy about this. I saw the way she looked, when her father was around, and I could tell she wanted to be far away from him. I was running out of time, and needed to go asap, I had to drop something off at the empire then head out of town. I was not even going, to see my father today fuck that! I gave Ms. Alice her number, and what school we go to and headed out.

Once I hit the highway, I did 80 all the way to the airport and was in deep thought. I arrived, and I parked my car, I got out, grabbing my bags. I locked my doors, heading inside just in time, pulled out my ticket. As I waited in line, I pulled out my phone, sending my baby a text. I tried calling Abbey, but got no answer, once again, and my gut was telling me something wrong. I gave the lady my ticket, and headed to get on the plane, I texted my mother and told her I loved her. Taking my seat on the plane, I relaxed my mind for a bit.

I really needed a break from all this, and was getting ready to say fuck the empire, and everything else. My pops was in the streets so much that he was not around us, and Aden turned out to be just like his ass. Faheem and I had dreams, which was going to college, him becoming a football player, and me graduating with a bachelor's degree in business administration.

Which was another reason why my father wanted me to oversee the empire. I did not want shit to do with this shit and was why I left before. Aden ass needed help, and I was going to give, him that fucking help. I am always there to help, his ass only to get stabbed in the back by him. Honestly, it stung bad, and I never thought my little brother would be the one who tries to kill me. I do not know what I did to him, wait I know I did not, do shit to him. His bitch ass just wanted to have his way, and bitch I'm not pops, he was playing with the right one.

Chapter 5
Abbey

"Abbey" My father annoying voice yelled

"Yes daddy" I said trying to sound sweet

"Come here now" he yelled again

I got up going into the hall, to see what he wanted, and I needed to pee badly. He was slowly walking up the steps, and I became irritated, trying to hold it in. I wished his old ass would hurry up, and walk faster, this nigga was pissing me off, like what the hell wrong with him.

"Dad I need to use the bathroom bad" I said ,shaking my leg

It seems he took a little longer;since I said that, I walked off going into the bathroom. Once I was done I washed my hands, and dried them on the hand towel, I walked out to see my father was at the top of the stairs pissed off.

"Bitch did I tell you to move" he hissed at me

"But daddy…."

I only got out before, he pushed me down all 24 steps, the pain shot up my side, and I couldn't take any more. He came down the steps faster then, he walked up them bitches, and bent down to my level. He smiled at me like, he loved the pain look on my face, he climbed on top of me, and began raping me. He went harder, and harder as I screamed out in pain, he took my virginity, and this feeling would change me for the rest of my life. He started choking me as he began talking,

"Abbey why are you fucking with me!! I've had a bad day, and don't mind whooping your ass"

"Damn you feel good baby girl, your mother has nothing on you!!!"

I looked for something to hit him with but there was nothing I could use, I was going to die I thought as I was beginning to lose my breath. I really hated my father, now and could not take it, I wanted him dead, and I was going to kill him myself.

Alice

"Today is the day!! You are finally free from this hell hole" Jane said smiling

"You think she would forgive me" I asked upset

"Only god knows!! Go see your daughter and explain" Jane said hugging me

I know you think I'm messed up for leaving Abbey with Ron, but I had no choice, and had my reasons. Her father was a cop, and I was just another girl to him, he got me locked up in this hell hole. When Ron and I first met he was just becoming a cop with his best friend Harrison, for all the wrong reasons if you asked me, and the beatings were worse. Ron beat me day in, and day out, and when I did not do what he asked, or late doing it he beat me. He was a very spiteful man, that his own family did not want shit to do with him. Ron's mother told me I needed to get out, before it got worse, but he kept me there. After I had Abbey he took her, and told the whole town I was unstable drunk and couldn't take care of my child. I got put in rehab for my drinking problems, and went to jail for five months, behind something he did. He got to keep Abbey; I needed a better mindset messing with Ron. Being back In Trenton brings back a lot of good and bad memories, walking out the train station I caught a cab to the last known address I could remember. I jump out the cab looking around, when I spot Aaron, putting bags in his trunk. I ran up on him, and he pulled out a gun. He pointed the gun at me, as he stared like he saw a ghost, my mind started to wonder.

"Ms. Alice?" He asked with his head tilted

"Yes boy!! Now where is Abbey?" I question him

"You're on the wrong side of town" he said jumping in his truck

"SHIT" I hissed out

He gave me a paper with her number and the name of her school, he gave me a hug, and said nice seeing you before he disappeared in his truck. I pulled out my phone calling her number, but only got the voicemail. I started to walk down the street when I bumped into someone falling to the ground. I looked up to see Harrison staring down at him, this smile came across his, and I knew it wasn't a good one either.

"Ron going to love to hear, you're back in town" he said

"Where are they" I hissed at him getting up

"I'm not telling you that, but I could tell you that we are treating the girls just right. You know like how we treated you, and your sister" he laughed walking away

He walked off, and I just stared at him as my blood boiled, now that Ron would be expecting me I had to come up with a better plan. I needed to save not just Abbey, but Bailey too. My sister and I did not grow up together, so when we finally saw each other again, we were with these fools. Our girls did not meet until the fourth grade because they kept us far away from each other. I wished time after time, that I listened to Ron's mother, she warned me, and I was too stupid to not listen. He had me wrapped around his fingers and that is not what I wanted for Abbey. When I was locked up, I found out my sister passed away, and I knew who did it. I was going to find Abbey and Bailey, and save them from what we dealt with, hope I wasn't too late.

I was so deep in thought that, I didn't realize I was at the fucking, hotel already. I signed in getting my keys, making my way to room 345, fourth floor. Stepping off the elevators, I walked down the hall, to my room.

Chapter 6
Bailey

As I sat in my room on my bed I waited for Farrah and Abbey to come so we could go out to check on things for my baby Aaron. I pulled out my phone, calling Abbey but got the voicemail multiple times. I began to worry when I heard my father's conversation.

"Aye Ron, Alice back in town looking for the girls" my father spoke loudly

"Look Harrison, calm down, you don't want Bailey to hear you. No one knew they were sisters, shit our kids do not even know, they are really cousins. I will handle Alice" Mr. Ron said a little irritated

"Farrah here, we will talk later" my father said again

"Alright one" Ron said one last time

I couldn't believe what I was hearing right now, all this time we were related, and it made sense as to why Abbey and I favored each other. My door flew open and my heart began pounding a little faster, my only thoughts was my father knew I heard his conversation.

"Hey girl!! Why you are looking like that" Farrah asked sitting down

"Where is Abbey?" I asked

"She never showed up to my house or answered the phone" Farrah stated

We waited a while longer, but she still never showed up. We went to the party without her. I didn't really want to; because I could not count on Farrah, wild ass to do it, she would have gotten drunk and forgot why she was there. We made it to the party to see everyone all over the place,
We made our way inside spotting them right away. I went to grab a soda and Farrah a shot of Remy, we sat watching them for a while. I could not understand why Aden hated Aaron so much, and Faheem became so innocent. From the looks of things Aaron made sure his brothers were always set, and was there when they got into some trouble. They spotted us, and made their way over to us, taking a deep gulp from my soda. They took a seat. Everything about Aden seemed wrong and had this evil side, Faheem was nothing like him. He got straight A's, and Aaron was the big brother who was always

there to lean on.

Aden

I knew how Aaron felt about Bailey especially after they fucked, so I was going to use her to get back at him, he took shit to far, and had it coming embarrassing a real nigga at school. Bailey had blue eyes attractively tousled red hair, she had this silver necklace around her neck with a locket on it, and she had a narrow but plum figure. I do not think his punk ass should oversee the empire, just because he was the oldest didn't mean shit, and his rules were worse than pops. Since my father trusted little old Aaron so much, I took what I needed from the trap house. I started my own empire, trying to take my own brother down. He treated me well, and always made sure I was cool, but his ass was mad fucking annoying. Aaron and I always bumped heads because I will never listen to him, I was the hot head where Aaron was the brain, and Faheem smart and calm. I watched as Farrah and Faheem left together, and I put my plan into motion.

"So, Bailey, are you not drinking?" I asked her to get closer

"Naw I'm good bro" she said shaking her head

"Well can I get you a soda?" I asked smiling

"Yea I guess," she said scrunching up her face

I walked off grabbing a soda for her, pulling the pills out of my pocket. I dropped one in her soda, Clever walked up on me, and I got pissed off. He was loyal to my brother only, and I couldn't do shit about it.

"Aye man what are you doing?" He asked looking around me

'Nothing Neff!! Now get your big ass out the way, and mind your

business" I snapped out at him

He stared at me for a while before walking off, clever really got under my skin because I could never get him to do shit I wanted like Aaron did, I knew he was here watching me for Aaron. Walking back over to Bailey, I handed her the soda, she took sips, and I smiled at her leaning over to try and kiss her.

"WHAT THE FUCK ADEN" she hissed at me

She got up looking around for Farrah, and when she spotted them, she made her way over there. I can hear her mention how I tried to kiss her, and she was going home in the uber. I followed behind her and watched as she waited for her uber to pull up, 30mins later her uber never arrived so I offered the ride home. She disagreed at first, but then soon later agreed, and we jumped in my truck. As I made my way down the highway, I saw her starting to doze off. I watched her blink her eyes a couple of times, her words were in a slur, and I got hyped for what was about to go down. I pulled into the parking by the football field, moving us to the back, I began fucking her.

She was so tight, and I loved it, pulling out my phone and I began recording it. Once I was done, I took her home, dropped her off, I carried her to her room, quietly and laid her down before making my way out the house. Looking around I made sure no one saw me because if her father was home my ass would be dead . Once I left, I began, cleaning up my tracks, and making sure I had alibis set up. I turned out to be just, like my father and I think, it is what bothered Aaron the most. Once I arrived home I began, cleaning my truck out, making sure there was nothing left behind.

Bailey

"What the fuck!! My head is killing me, but I didn't drink anything"

"How the fuck did I even, get home I don't remember coming in"

I sat there talking to myself, I couldn't wrap my mind around all this, I pulled out my phone calling Farrah. She did not answer, so I got up making my way to the bathroom feeling sick. My head was spinning, so I took two Advil, I stripped and jumped in the shower. The hot water ran down, my body and I got relaxed, the last thing I remembered was getting in the car with Aden. After I got out of the shower, I wrapped the towel around me, going into my room. Sitting on my bed I began to have flashbacks, I could see these bright lights, like I was by a football field or something. As I tried to think more, my head began to hurt. I got dressed laying back down, to relax my mind a bit, I could not wait to talk to Aaron.

Closing my eyes, I see Aden on top of me, but I could not move, jumping up I opened my eyes with my mind racing. As I began to put the pieces together I felt nasty, I needed to ask around, and see who saw him. I throw my shoes on, grabbing my phone, heading towards the door. I reached the bottom to see my father and Mr. Ron talking. I wanted to know where Abbey was, but I would not dare ask them fools. I spoke to them, as I walked out the door, as I walked down the street I see, everybody staring at me, it was something I was used to, but it was more than usual. I spotted Faheem standing outside the football field, making my way over to him, he looked at me, and we began talking. I really needed to know, what the fuck going on.

"What's up, Bailey!! Are you good?" He asked

"What happened last night?" I asked him

"You left early because Aden tried to kiss you" He said looking at me wired

"Are you sure you are ok? I would've thought that you, would have remembered, since your drunk soda all night" He said again

I turned around leaving fast, as the flashbacks came back all at once, "Bailey" Faheem called out, but I kept it moving. Running out the field, I made my way home, not needing any more answers, I got the urge to throw up. I made my way to the trash can, bending over I began, throwing up. After I was done emptying my stomach in the trash I remembered the soda, thoughts from that came ,again I saw what happened and could not believe Aden did that to me. I did not know what to think or how would I tell Aaron any of this. My phone made a sound, pulling it out, I quickly noticed it was an unsaved number and I wondered.

Opening the text, I see a video of me, Aden was on top of me having his way, the last piece to the puzzle came flushing back and I fainted. I could hear people running my way, I could hear Faheem, screaming my name, but for the life of me I could not move or respond. As the sirens got louder, I began passing out again. I woke up to a machine hooked up to me, laying in the hospital bed, looking over I see Faheem, sitting in the chair. He was so busy on the phone, trying to calm whoever down, that he did not notice I was awake. A nurse came in, and began checking me, her voice was soft and calming.

"Hi Bailey!! I'm nurse Sammie" she said

"I'll be right back sis ok" Faheem said walking out still on the phone"

"Well Bailey I have good news, and bad news for you "she said

"What's the bad news?" I asked without looking up

"Bad news is, you were drugged with a date rap pil,l" she said fast

"I couldn't believe, Aden drugged me"

"Good news?" I asked her

"Well you're pregnant with twins!!" She said happily

I just sat there, with you nothing to say, my mind drifted to all things.

Aaron took my virginity and Aden drugs me, oh let us not forget, the twins. What the hell was I going to do? I still had time to get out of my father's house before he found out and let us pray they did not call him. The nurse walked out, and I kept thinking, I blinked my eyes and opened them to see the unexpected.

Chapter 7
Abbey(2 weeks later)

Ever since my father pushed me down all these stairs, and rapped me I was stuck in my room, with the door locked. I will never be the same, after what he did to me, and it hurts how he just takes my innocence away. I wanted out of this bad situation and could not wait until I went off to college. I have been ignoring everyone's calls, and texts because I do not want to turn my phone on. I wished my mother was around during shit like this. I have not been to school, or anything. My body felt so nasty. The loud bang on my door made me jump out in fear, and tears began rolling down my face. I was honestly scared for my life right now, and did not know what I should do.

"ABBEY IF I HAVE TO KICK, THIS DOOR DOWN YOU WILL REGRET IT" he hissed from the other side of the door.

The banging continued, and I began crying praying for help, my door flew off the hedging, and I jumped up in fear. He got closer to me, and backhanded me, making me fall to the ground hard, grabbing my face. I see the blood coming from my face. Trying to get up he jumped on me, knocking me back down, he pulled down my sweatpants, and panties forcing himself inside me once again. Crying out in pain, he went faster, the knock on the front door did not faze, him at all, and he continued to ram himself inside of me

. "WHY ME GOD!!! JUST TAKE ME NOW" I cried between tears

He smacked me across the face again, and I started to become numb to the hits to come. Once he finished having his way with me, he got up leaving the room, and I laid there not able to move. I forced myself to get up. and made my way to the bathroom, I locked the door behind me going to the tub and sitting. My body was in so much pain, and I knew for a fact a man would never touch me in that way again, nor did I trust any nigga anymore. I was going to break free, even if I had to kill him myself, because this shit was taking a toll on me. I sat in the tub in pure hot water washing my father's dirty sins off me. There was more than just hate I had built up for him. I wanted to take him out with no regret, I believed in God and prayed he would help me out of this. I had no family or no one to turn to for that matter, so I continued to sit in the water after scrubbing my body clean for like the 20th time. My phone began ringing off the hook, and I wondered how the shit even got cut back on, I stepped out the tub wrapping my towel around me letting the water out. Walking out of my bathroom to go into my room I see the mess my father made was cleaned up, his deep annoying voice made me jump and I looked up to see him standing there smiling hard as hell.

"HURRY THE FUCK UP AND GET DRESSED THE GIRLS WILL BE HERE SOON" he said licking his lips.

I quickly grabbed my clothes and went back into the bathroom with my heart basically in my hands, hurrying to put my clothes on I looked in the mirror noticing how fucked up I looked. Standing in the mirror I tried to cover up on the bruises my father made, the ones on my thighs I covered with sweat pants and I put makeup on to cover up the cut on my face from him backhanding me. I walked out of my bathroom and just sat at the edge of the bed thinking I was scared for my life more, so many thoughts went through my head it was crazy. I wondered when I will be free from the beatings and now the rape, this shit was talking really taking a toll on me that I started crying again.

"Hey, Ab, you're OK? Aaron asked about you" Bailey said sitting next to me.

I scooted over to the other side of the bed and began talking staring into space, I just wanted to be free and do not want anyone to have it as hard as me right now.

"Abbey are you OK? You been kind of distant lately "Farrah asked

"Hey I'm fine yawl!! So, what's been up" I said trying to put joy in my voice

"I'll be back" Farrah said leaving out

Bailey and I sat in silence for a while before any of us began speaking, from the look on her face I knew something happened to her also. She did not really like talking around Farrah which I understood because Farrah wild ass claims we are extra sometimes. Farrah's dad loved her gave her ass whatever but not like Mr. Harrison and my father did us.

"Bailey what's wrong" I asked her

"That night we went to check on the boys for Aaron something happened" she said exceptionally low.

"What do you mean boo?" I asked her

"The last thing I remember is Aden driving me home, but I never had a drink of anything, and my head was pounding the next morning. I do not even remember walking through that door or anything. I had flashbacks and woke up in the hospital, to find out I was pregnant with twins.

Let us not forget Aden drugged me" she said a little lower

"Wait what Bailey who I need to fuck up and did you tell Aaron" I asked rubbing her back

"No, I'm scared boo" she said, tearing up.

"I'll go with you but I have some tea to spill to, my father been raping me" I said crying now.

"WHAT THE FUCK AB" she semi yelled

"I know I should have told yawl but how can I just come out and say that, you know how Farrah ass is" I said honestly

"Look boo you're my best friend I got your back while you got my front, what you trying to kill these niggas finally?" she said pacing the floor

"I plan to trust me," I said, shaking my head.

Farrah walked in with a bag full of shit and I got hyped for the snacks to come, Farrah wild ass means well but she gets her way most times with her dad until my father steps in and says he needs to be a stronger man. We sat on my bed in Indian style and ate snacks while talking, I ended up telling her what my father did, and she screamed aloud. she had secrets of her own to spill. Farrah always made sure she did not tell what was going on at her house but was quick to judge us saying we are extra.

Aaron

I just made it back to town, and could not wait to see my baby. Faheem said she was in the hospital but could not say why. I wonder how shit went at the party. Clever told me that he seen, Farrah and

Bailey there, but Abbey was not which was wired. They were like three peas in a pod. I got off the plane heading out the door. Once I finally reached outside, I looked for my car, spotting it and I made my way over to it. Unlocking my doors, I quickly throw my bags in the back seat. I jumped in the driver's side speeding off, the trip went well, and everything was handled. My mind was made up, after that I was done, with this shit, Aden could fucking have it. I am not about to fight, my little brother over, something I give two shits about, our father only trusted my ass because of my degree. As I came to a red light I pulled out my phone, I had an all-black Dodge Dart, my phone ranged throughout the car as I sped off. It ranged a couple more times, but Faheem ass did not, answer "what the fuck" I thought out loud. I tried calling Bailey, and she answered, on the second ring, that's my baby. I think I might love that girl.

"Hey baby!! What's up" she said happily

"Nothing much love, what you are doing" I said turning a corner

"Nothing walking with Abbey, on our way to the store she about to cook" she said again

"Tell Abbey I want a plate, and we need to talk" I said looking around

"Your house like old times?" Abbey asked through the phone

"His ass is still out of town girl!!" My baby said laughing

"My house is like old times! "I said laughing

We talked a little more, before hanging up, and just as I was turning to the coroner, I spotted them crossing the street. I watched as they walked by with the bags talking, something seemed different, about them both, and I wanted to know what. What the fuck could, of happened in these, last two weeks, I beeped the horn rolling down my window. They noticed it was me and jumped in, I sped off going to my house.

"Abbey, I've been trying to call you what's up sis?" I said looking through the mirror

"Aaron, I really don't know how to explain, no one would believe me anyway" she said looking out the window tearing up

"What happened? Because something up, with yawl both"" I said a little upset that I wasn't there for them

"I've never lied to you, you're like a big brother to me, so I will be honest. About two weeks ago, my father started raping me, and I could not do shit about it. Which was why I couldn't come To the party to help watch Aden" she said very upset now crying

"Now can I kill him, you're not going back there", I said pissed off driving fast as hell

It got quiet for a little while, and out of the corner of my eye, I saw Bailey shift in her seat, when Aden's name was mentioned, she started looking out the window. When I was about to ask, Abbey began snapping out, and I understood why. I couldn't believe, her dad would do some, shit like that but then he looks like the type

"Where the fuck, I'm going to stay? and where I'm getting clothes from? I want to kill him myself" She said to me with no emotions

"You're my sister, I got a place for you so chill out, your wish is my command. I will set something up and let you know. oh, shit did you see your mom?" I said to her

"My mom?" She questioned me

"Yeah that's why I been calling you" I said shaking my head

"Speaking of that Abbey, I overheard our dads, and Ron was upset that she was back. Oh, and our mothers were sisters, we are cousins" Bailey said

We talked more as I drove to my house, and my mind was stuck, in the same place. I was gone for only two weeks, and all this shit happened. I pulled up to my house to see Ms. Alice sitting there, looking back at Abbey, I could see her starting to tear up. I parked my car, and we all got out, Ms. Alice ran to Abbey trying to hug her tightly, but Abbey pushed her away. Ms. Alice began to cry, and Abbey walked away, they haven't seen each other in years, so I understood.

Ms. Alice said she was going to go and I unlocked the door so Abbey and Bailey could go inside. I stood outside to talk to Ms. Alice for a minute but she wouldn't stay long. She passed me this envelope and said give it to her daughter. I said ok and with that, she left so I headed inside to the girls in the kitchen getting ready to cook, I headed upstairs, to get changed. Faheem texted saying, he wanted to meet up, and I agreed, going into my room I headed for the shower. Once I was done, with my 30-minute shower, I headed to my room and got dressed. I threw on my all navy Nike GX Fleece Tracksuit, with my all black high tops. As I made my way down stairs I could smell the food, and it was smelling good. I walked in to see them mixing up the baked mac and cheese ready to put in the oven. I told them I would be back and headed out to meet up with Faheem.Jumping, in my car speeding down the driveway, I turned left going to my mother house. I arrived about 30 minutes later, and parked heading inside. My mother house was trashed what the fuck happened here, I thought looking around. I walked into the living room to see my mother, terribly upset and she knew whoever did this. I sat down next to my mother and

Faheem walked in, going off about what happened.

"You tell him, when I catch him, I'm fucking him up, Aaron is the least of his worries" he said hanging up

He looked at me, and calmed down. He explained to me what happened to our mother house. Aden fucked up the house, because our mother would not, give him 150 dollars towards some bullshit. I made my mother stop giving him money. He had plenty of money but decided to use hers. She gave him whatever just to keep him happy. our mother stressed over him daily. I helped clean up the house before heading home. I was going to whoop, the living shits out of him. About 30 mins later, we were done, I gave our mother a kiss, telling her I will be back. I walked out jumping into my car, doing 70 in a 50-mile zone. Once I arrived, I parked, going straight in. Opening the front door, I could hear their conversation, and it made me madder than what I already was. I could hear Bailey saying how Aden drugged her and raped her and, that she was pregnant with twins. Hearing all this I got pissed off, Aden ass was really getting under my skin now, I knocked the trophy over, making everyone look back at me. I was not mad at Abbey or Bailey, just wished they told me this shit. I started putting two and two together, and it all started to make sense. I jumped back in my car calling Clever. He said we should meet up, and I agreed to make my way there.

Chapter 8
Farrah

As I finished my last date, in the VIP room I walked out, looking back making sure, I did not leave shit behind. Walking to get my things, from the back, I see Aaron, Clever and Faheem walk in. My heart rate sped up, and I was slowly losing my breath, but I had to man up fast or else my ass was grassed. Now my life was not so perfect, like Abbey and Bailey thought, I mean my parents are awesome, but this dude Mark I met is a problem. Abbey and Bailey thought my parents bought all the shit I have but they did not. Mark and I met one, night at this party over a blunt he offered to share, he became my dealer and someone I was fucking.

We started to get involved with each other, I became a heavy smoker, but I only found out, my blunts were laced. I got hooked badly, and he convinced me to start stripping to pay for my habit, for him only to take all my money I made. Now I was not there stripping at all, I did private dates in the VIP rooms, I was always high as a kite, and never really knew what to expect from these niggas. My phone began ringing off the hook, looking at it I saw Mark, name going across the screen, I quickly picked up and shit got deep.

"Who the fuck are you hiding from Hun!!! I know damn well you not messing with none of those niggas, I will fuck you up bitch" he hissed through the phone

"Look calm down, I was done, and I have all your money, so when can I get that blunt" I pleaded with him

"Let's fucking go now!!!" He said hanging up

I quickly jumped up, grabbing all my things, heading out so I could meet Mark, I made my way through everyone, when my name got called. Looking over I see Aaron, telling me to come over, and on the other side Mark stood there pissed. I knew he would not be happy about this shit at all, but those are my friends, and god knows I do not need Abbey and Bailey to know. I took a seat, and everyone looked at me, the look on Aaron's face, told me he was pissed, he was like a big brother to me and I couldn't lie to him.

"Well hey to you too!!" Faheem said rolling his eyes

"What the fuck!!!" Aaron shouted

"Look I can explain, please calm down" I pleaded with him

"Yes, Farrah please explain" he said looking at me

As I sat there, I wondered what the hell I was going to tell him, because he always knew when our ass was lying. I began fixing my lips, to talk when Mark walked up, he grabbed me by the arm, making Aaron and them jump up. They looked at me, and I closed my eyes, Faheem looked kind of hurt, and the pain from it struck me inside. Aaron was pissed, and disappointed in me, I just couldn't stand it, Mark whispered in my ear and I got scared.

"Farrah, what the fuck" Aaron shouted out

"Aaron, I'm sorry!!" I said tearing up

"Oh, it's so good, to put a name with the face, Aden was right about you" Mark laughed

"What the fuck you say?" Aaron questioned

"Farrah let's go," Mark said walking off

"I'll see you real soon" Aaron yelled out

Once we got to his house, he started yelling, I ran around the room so, he wouldn't hit me, the niggas heavy-handed as hell. I got tired of running around in circles, so I fell to the bed letting him have his way. My mind drifted to how, everyone hated me, and disappointed in me, Mark ass turned me into someone I barely even knew. I look in the mirror, and don't know the girl, looking back at me.

I woke up to him, pulling up my skirt, ramming himself inside my ass, the pain was unbearable, and the more I fought, the harder he went. He turned me around, and rammed my pussy, I was so sore, and my body was aching bad. I knew I could not go see, my parents looking, fucked up like this, I will never hear the end of it. I needed a way out of this shit, but how will I get, that because this nigga crazy.

He got up, went into the bathroom, and I couldn't move. I wanted to get up, and walk out of here. I felt Abbey and Bailey pain. I always thought they were overreacting until I happened to be in the same situation. I knew for sure they would be disappointed in me because this was not Farrah, my parents gave birth too. Mark changed me in ways, I would have never thought.

It was almost like he had some kind of spell on me, and I listened like a dummy, I had this job to do, and it was something to do, with me killing if I have too, for money and I wasn't with it honestly. I felt like all these damn robberies were going to catch up to me, then there was this job I had to do today, in Vegas with my homegirl from the club. I tried to get up, and this time I succeeded. Mark made his way over to me kissing me, he then apologized but I couldn't take him seriously, until he passed me that blunt.

I walked pass him going, into the bathroom, looking in the mirror, my face was fucked, up and I had a lot of work to do. I turned the hot water on, and let it run for a little, before getting in. Mark ass always tried to butter me up, after whooping my ass, the night before; but I always fell for it as long as I was getting my next fix.

Once I was done, with my shower I began covering up all my bruises, and scars using my makeup. I quickly put the makeup on, making sure every scar was covered up, looking in the mirror one last time I head back to the room. Mark ass sat patiently, waiting for me to get dressed, he relit the blunt passing it to me, taking long deep pulls I took it all in and in no time, I was high as a kite.

"Here baby!! Take this with you" he said passing me a gun

"What's this for?" I asked holding it

"Making sure you protected bay" he said licking his lips

As I was done getting dressed my phone began ringing off the hook, Shelly ass called back to back, picking it up I mentioned I was on my way before hanging up. I put my last touches on before heading out, I reached my car heading to the place. I arrived to see Shelly ass waiting on me, I parked getting out greeting her, and we made our way in. My palms get sweaty, and I got nervous as shit,

All we had to do tonight was get him drunk, and take his money, we approached the bar, and the game began. He passed us drinks, and we began talking, his Caramel skin complexion, and blue eyes made him more attractive. We sat at the bar for at least 2 hours, he licked his lips, letting me know he was ready to get down, and we made our way to his room.

We reached his room and he unlocked the door; we all went in and I took a seat, he began pouring, us some henny and the party began. He sat down, and he began talking while rubbing Shelly's legs, she got on top of him and I got up looking around. He was so into it that he didn't even see me move, she did her job and I did mine.

As Shelly did her thing, I went into the bathroom, and started searching for the money. Under the sink in the trash can, there sat 1000$. I grabbed it, sticking it in my purse, walking back in the room I saw him knocked out with Shelly's ass on top of him. I woke her up telling her to let's go and thought about how this job was easier than I *could imagine.*

Shelly reached in the drawer grabbing all his jewelry, when she was done, we tiptoed to the door and soon we made it he woke up. My heart rate sped up and I got scared as hell, he began raising his voice while Shelly and I backed up against the door.

"What the fuck going on here?" He yelled

"Please calm down we just leaving" Shelly pleaded

"Give me my shit and get the fuck out" he hissed at us

He began walking over to us and I pulled out the gun pointing it at him, he still walked over to us and I didn't know what to do. The more he got closer the more I got scared out of fear, my hands trembled, and the gun went off, looking over at Shelly we both stood there out of shock. His body fell to the ground and the blood poured out on the hotel floor, he soon stopped breathing and I quickly stuck the gun back in my purse, we ran out without looking back. Once we got outside, I began taking deep breaths. I couldn't believe I just killed someone, jumping in my car, we sped off going back home, my mind was clouded, and I couldn't stand the feeling of what just happened. As I sped down the highway my mind kept drifting to what happened. I missed my best friends a lot, but I couldn't tell them about this life I was living.

"Farrah are you ok?" Shelly asked me with a worried look

"Yeah I'm fine" I said looking back at the road

We drove a couple more hours before we made it home, my mind was shot, and my high was gone, I needed another fix or something stronger. Dropping Shelly off I headed home, I walked in the house to *see Mark sitting there and I passed him everything I had. He looked from me to the money and jewelry, then back to me as he got up walking towards me. With every step he made, he took another gulp of the beer and my mind raced to what was about to happen. I knew for sure he was mad because I did not get enough money tonight, we were standing face to face when he smacked me. I fell to the ground hard and my mind went back to dude I just killed for this money, Mark ass bent down to my level and began kissing me, I pushed him off and he looked at me crazy.*

He got up sitting on the edge of the bed, he pulled out a blunt and my eyes were glued, he looked at me as I looked at the blunt getting up, he mentioned for me to come over and I did as was told. We sat on the bed as he got on top of me, he looked me in the eyes. He lit the blunt passing it to me, and I got high as a kite and just then all my worries went out the window. Once Mark fell asleep, I wanted to get some food because his house never has shit, this nigga never goes shopping with his stupid ass. I got up heading out the door, grabbing the blunt to take with me, I sat in the car thinking for a while. I really miss Bailey and Abbey, but they could not see me like this, as I lit the blunt, I began taking long pulls in hailing deep pulls. I got out of the car going back inside to be greeted by Mark's hit, I fell to the ground and I thought about how tired I was of all this.

Getting up I went into the living room, looking in the mirror I saw my lip busted, Mark ass came up behind me and started choking me. I could not keep letting him do this trying to find air between him choking me. I looked over to see his trophy there. I grabbed it, hitting him upside the head and he fell to the ground hard, checking to see if he was breathing, I noticed it was slowly fading away. I grabbed my keys running out of the house not looking back, I pulled out my phone calling Abbey and she answered right away.

"Abbey, I need you to meet me somewhere please" I said quickly

"Ok where" she said worried

"Our old hang out place" I said hanging up

I pulled off full speed still high as a kite, as I drove down the streets my mind drifted to how I killed two men and I couldn't believe what was happening to me. Getting mixed up with Mark was the worst part of my life. I made it to the highway, and I joined the traffic which was a lot of it, shit I hated being stuck in traffic on the highway at that. As I am driving, I began smoking this black, flashbacks of both murders I committed started coming back. Putting the black out I began focusing back on the road, but the flashbacks only came back, and it was like I was living it all over again, trying to focus on the road I couldn't and before I knew it a truck hit me.

Chapter 9
Abbey

We waited for hours but Farrah never showed up. I called her a couple of times but only got no answer and I started to worry and we left. As we drove back to Aaron's house, we saw the highway blocked off, there was an accident and I prayed it was not Farrah. We went the other way and headed to the house and I couldn't get my mind off how she sounded, I hoped she was ok because honestly, I haven't seen her in a while and the last time I heard anything was really when Aaron mentioned seeing her.

My phone began ringing and it was my father calling, and I didn't answer it, but I must admit I got scared looking through my mirrors. Shit for all I know he was one of those cops out there just now, he called a couple more times and I was convinced he seen my car and I got scared as fuck. Once we reached the house Bailey went straight in *and I sat in the car listening to my father voicemails.*

"Abbey, I know you see my damn calls, you better get the hell home because if I have to find you it's going to be bad on you" he hissed

Putting my phone away I went inside joining everyone, We had school tomorrow and I prayed that Farrah show up because we needed to make plans for graduation. I pulled out my laptop and began looking online for something to wear, Aaron told me to do this weeks ago but I'm just getting to it of course, Aaron came walking in, he sat down on the sofa and started talking about graduation I was happy as hell because I get to move out this messed up town and be far away from my father ass, I wasn't going to tell them he tried to call me or anything like that and I wasn't going to answer any of his calls.

Faheem brought their mother, Ms. Roselee came over and she disappeared somewhere in the kitchen. Aaron and Faheem stood in the hall talking about Aden ass and I continued to look at stuff online. Bailey's belly was slowly growing. I had to find her something nice. Being pregnant with twins is hard on her and I am here for her through it all, it is a good thing Aaron is sticking by her side.

"Yawl ready for this college life?" Faheem asked us smiling

"I'm going to be big as shit" Bailey said laughing

"We not staying on campus anyway" I mentioned

"The turn up going to be so real" Faheem said hyped up

"Aye" I yelled

We talked about college more and I couldn't wait to get there for a fresh start, my phone began ringing again making everyone look at me and I only noticed it was my father once again. I was happy not getting abused and raped by my father at the moment changed my mind about dudes in way I never thought, like I found out ,Clever has a crush on me, but I would not dare get that close. My father damaged me in a way that I could not come close to anyone besides Faheem and Aaron only because they were like brothers to me. I was going to be a lonely ass with mad cats running around and no kids, but I truly prayed god would heal me from this mess. My phone began ringing again. and I throw it across the room seeing my father's name go across the screen. I got up going to my room because I just wanted to be alone and what he did to me always haunts me.

2 Days Later

Walking down the school halls I couldn't believe how much shit has changed in so little time, like Bailey begin my blood cousin and her being pregnant with twins and so on. The kids here are still fucked up and ratchet as hell and all the name calling was pass me, we made it to the gym to practice for graduation and I could not believe I made it this far. After practice we made our way home and I looked over my shoulder the whole way there. I had this feeling deep down in my gut that my father was close by and I did not want to see him. I was afraid of what he might do to me and most of all I knew what he could do to me and whoever else tried to stop him.

Once we made it home Bailey went off to start getting stuff ready for tomorrow because it was the day our ass will be free from this fucked up town but before I went to get my stuff ready I decided to look over what my mother gave me. I sat on my bed and opened up the envelope my mother gave me. There were a bunch of papers as I read over each one I noticed my mother got locked up and you wouldn't *believe who the arresting officer was. She then had to go to rehab dam so she did not just up and leave me.*

After reading over all my mother papers I feared my father would show up to the graduation with no regrets even if he acted a fool. I just wanted this day to go by, so we can be in another state already. I wanted to be a doctor, lawyer and a social worker so I had my hands full, but I will push through this all, I wanted to save those kids from stuff like what I was through. I laid in my bed with thoughts floating around in my head.

Bailey and I sat up for hours talking while she did our hair, she was very good at it and I loved the way she always hooked me up. My mom came in and she sat down to talk and explain everything that wasn't on those papers, so we just had a girl's night in my room I had to give her a chance to explain at least, Bailey had a doctor's appointment tomorrow after graduation for a Paternity Test which was a big risk but I'm here for her through it all.

My phone started ringing off the hook and I saw this unknown number showing up, my heart rate sped up thinking my father was using someone else's phone to get in contact with me. Picking it up I hear the people in the background screaming cold blue and I wondered what the hell was going on. Saying hello the nurse began speaking and I got stuck and couldn't say anything or move. I really prayed that she was ok only to find out she was injured badly.

"Hi this is nurse Ashley and I'm calling on behalf of Farrah Morris she has you an emergency contact along with her parents who I couldn't reach, I'm calling because she been in a bad accident and there's a chance she can go into a coma so if you can get down here fast please she been asking about you and a Bailey" the lady soft voice spoke

Not saying another word, I got up and began getting dressed my heart rate speed up, most of all I couldn't believe this was happening and I would have never thought she out of all people would be going through this but as they say don't judge a book by its cover, my mother and Bailey didn't ask any questions they just went and got ready also.

Once we were already we headed out to go visit Farrah I couldn't get my mind off how she would look because that was a pretty bad accident on that highway, the damn car got hit by a eighteen-wheeler truck, so I was now praying for my friend, my mother rubbed my back as I drove, and the car was damn quiet. I made it there about ten minutes later and found a Park right away, looking back at everyone we prepared ourselves to go in. Once we got the room number we made our way to the elevators, we got on the elevator and my hands started to sweat and my mind kept thinking about Farrah like what the hell she got herself wrapped in.

Walking in her room the light was dimmed and she laid there watching tv wrapped up like a mummy would be, she was hurt badly and I felt for my friend I wished she was in better health because seeing her like this was killing me inside. I always knew she was a wild girl because when she did not listen to her mother, her mom would call me all the time and the other night she mentioned she hadn't seen her since she got mixed up with that boy. I wanted to know what the hell happened, what the fuck did this dude did to her and where can I find his ass? Her parents soon walked in and stuff soon got heated.

"I'm glad you came and its nice seeing you again Ms. Alice… mom and dad I know yall are very disappointed in me" Farrah spoke quietly not looking our way

"What the hell happened?" Bailey asked

"Look I know you all are disappointed in me and I have a lot of explaining to do, member that day yawl father came embarrassing yall in front of the school I wanted yawl to meet this guy. I thought he was nice and sweet, but I only soon found out it was all lies, he was lacing me blunts with heroin talked me into stripping, and he soon became my dealer before I knew it was getting laced it was too late I was already hooked, and I needed it every chance I get "she stopped talking

"Farrah!!" I said

"Farrah" Bailey said

"Farrah" her parents screamed

She didn't move or say anything. Soon the machines started going crazy and my heart dropped to the ground, the nurses ran in and we had to be removed from the room. I couldn't believe this was happening, she was there then she was gone just like that. We graduate tomorrow, and she will not be walking with us. Bailey and I looked at each other then back at the room before bringing each other into a tight hug. She was crying and so was I because most of all we couldn't believe this was happening to her, the nurse came out saying she fell into a coma and they don't know when she will wake up or if she will wake up, I walked off not able to hear any more of it.

Next Morning

I woke up the next morning with a lot of shit on my mind, I'm supposed to be getting ready for graduation but for the past thirty minutes I been stuck in this same spot, between Farrah going into a coma and my father constantly calling I didn't know where my mind was taking me, my mother came in looking at me and from the look on her face she felt my pain also. She sat next to me rubbing my back and it felt good to have her back, I couldn't explain to my mom what my father did to me, but she knows he beat me, the only people who know about the rape is Bailey, Farrah, and Aaron.

I was ashamed of telling that story and I wouldn't tell no one because who would believe me anyway? My phone started ringing and my father's name came across the screen. My heart dropped, and my mother just looked at me. I got up going into the bathroom to start getting ready, turning the hot water on. I locked the door and began praying that my father do not show up. I walked back into my room to see my mother gone and I began getting dressed in my black Lace Pleat Maxi Dress and some red wedges. I thanked Aaron over and over for this because I was killing it.

Making my way down stairs I watched my step and each step I took it clicked in my head how I fell down 24 damn steps, I took my mind off all the bad things and started to focus on what is ahead for me. I reached down stairs and see everyone waiting for me, Bailey wore this red lace high-low sleeveless dress with some black wedges and Faheem wore these black pants with his red collared dress shirt and tie, to complete his outfit he had his all red canvas and black blazer we were killing the shit right now, even though Farrah not here I was going keep her in spirit.

Clever came in looking like a snack and I had to turn around to stop the eye contact. I was blushing so hard, I didn't even know he went to our school and was graduating with us, and I assumed since he was Aaron's friend he was around his age. Aaron was older than us by two years, and he graduated last year and went off to college so Clever began his friend. I thought he had gone to college and all that good shit. Aaron and my mother took pictures of all of us before we headed out. Once we were on our way my phone began ringing off hook and I just knew my father was going to keep calling so I answered it. I just listened as he talked. I had no words to say, and I didn't want to be *anywhere near him.*

"Abbey, I don't know why you are fucking with me, do you know what I can do to you but listen sorry I won't be able to be attended the graduation because I have this big bust coming up, and if your ass not home about time I get there I will find you. Oh, and tell your mother I said hey she is looking really good!!" he said before hanging up

I just sat there in a daze because he was watching me like I thought he was, and he even knew I was with my mother. Now you see why I didn't trust my father because he always showed when you least expect it. It felt like no matter where I am at, he has me trapped. We arrived at the hall and I was happy as hell I couldn't wait to start college and get on out this fucked up town, we walked in and all eyes was on us I looked around and see Aden was not here I bet his ass wouldn't show but I know he would be at that damn after party. We took our seats and soon after the ceremony began, the principal talked so much with his boring ass voice that I started to get sleepy, after his long speech they began calling our names for our diplomas.

After he called a couple kids names he called Bailey name and I got hyped seeing her walk across the stage her belly was getting bigger from the twins, but she was killing it and then my mind drifted to Farrah. I so wished she were here with us like we planned but she is here with us through spirit and I will be getting the diploma for her. I was so deep in thought that I did not even hear my name being called until the boy behind me started tapping me, looking over I see clever looking at me like get your ass up. They called my name one last time and I got up to get my diploma and as I'm walking up they started to introduce all my achievements to the guest and rest of the class. They then brought up me being one of the top 5 students of the entire class of 2017 once I reached the principal and other staff. I shook their hands while pictures were taken of me and the staff. My mother was proud of me and it made me feel good inside. It felt good to say no *matter what my father did to me I kept faith and I made it through school and all.*

I went to the bathroom while everyone stood around talking because I had to go bad and I couldn't wait until they were done talking, I reached the bathroom going straight in and I reached the stall and began using the bathroom. Once I was done, I walked out to wash my hands at the sink, looking up in the mirror I saw my father standing behind me and my heart dropped. I knew I could not trust a word he says but why here? Why now? Didn't he hurt me enough, the smile that went across his face made me sick inside and I tried to leave. He grabbed me by the hair pulling me back and I screamed out in pain, he covered my mouth, so no one would hear me, and I began losing my breath a little before he let me go. I prayed he would not show up, but he did, and I felt the anger he had built up inside.

"Abbey, I don't know why you thought I was playing with you, I knew for a fact you weren't going to come home so I'll bring your ass home. Where your mom fine ass she can come too, and we could be a family again you know I missed your sweet ass" he said smiling

I felt nasty because I knew what he meant when he said my sweet ass, I would kill his ass before I ever let him touch me in that way again. I smacked his hands away from my thighs and he smacked me hard as hell, I fell to the ground grabbing my face. He put this rag over my face and I started to lose consciousness. My last thoughts before I passed out was why me. I woke up and it was dark as hell, not to mention I was no longer at the school, I got up looking around and noticed right away that I was back at this damn hell hole my father called home. I could hear his deep voice echo throughout the house, and I jumped at the sound of his voice, my body was aching with blood stains going down my legs and knew for sure he raped me again. Searching for my phone I couldn't find it but could hear it ringing, putting my ear to the room door. I see my father had my *phone and there wasn't shit I could do.*

Looking around my room I began searching for my tablet, throwing stuff around it wasn't where it used to be, so I left my room to go searching other places. My father was in the game room and I took the time to go the other way and search around, going down the steps his voice started to fade away, standing in the kitchen I pulled out the drawer grabbing a knife sticking in my pocket. Heading towards the front door I tried to open it but couldn't get out, it was like he had it locked with a code or some shit. I began to get frustrated. I banged on the door and my father soon came running down the steps. Before I could run off he grabbed me throwing me to the ground, he climbed on top of me and started hitting me, pulling out the knife I tried to stab him with, but he took the knife throwing it across the room.

Chapter 10
Aaron

Clever, Faheem and I searched all over for Abbey but what I couldn't understand was how did she just disappear from the school like that, it's been weeks and no one has heard or seen her. Clever has been in his feelings since it happened because the boy got a real big crush on her. Even though Abbey ass wouldn't give him the time of day; I had a meeting with my peoples who work the street and I needed to know what the hell the word is about Abbey. I walked down the street looking at my phone praying she texted me, I took her to be a little sister to me very seriously and I played the shit out of the role that you would've thought she was my real sister. Someone bumped into me making me drop my phone and keys, getting pissed I looked up to see Abbey and Bailey fathers staring at me. Grabbing my things off the ground I stood there looking at them, they had something up their sleeves and I wanted to know what, now they never liked my ass and really didn't have a reason why, but they worked with my father before on some shit I just didn't trust them.

"Hey Youngblood!!! How's everything?" Mr. Ron asked

"I'm good and you" I said looking them up and down

"How are your pops doing?" Mr. Harrison asked

"He is doing good, why you ask?" I asked with my head to the side now

"No reason" he said humping his shoulders

"How's Abbey and Bailey doing?" I asked knowing the answer already

Their bodies switched up and I could tell something was up with them, as I waited for them to answer my question I read their body language and I knew they knew where the hell Abbey was at. It clicked in my head how she said he raped her and my blood started to boil but I needed to play my cards right in case he did have her. My thoughts were broken when they started to speak, and I listened very carefully.

"They are doing fine, just graduated" Mr. Ron said not looking me in the eye

"Well tell them I said hi and I gotta go I'm running late" I said walking off

I walked in the spot to see everyone sitting waiting for me but not only that, my crew was here Bailey, Ms. Alice, Faheem and Clever sat on my right-hand side, I wasn't expecting them to be here but I'm glad they are. We sat at the table and began talking. They leave for college in two days and we were very worried about her. Meanwhile, I still had to deal with Aden ass still also, why not kill two birds and one stone.

They showed me this video of Aden drunk bragging about what he did to Bailey, Aden also mentioned how he's been working with Ron. I shifted in my seat and my blood began to boil. I honestly feel like that run in was a setup, I needed to get Faheem, Bailey and Abbey far away from this. Ms. Alice will go to watch over them there until I get there, Clever wanted to stay and help me but my little nigga had to go I wanted better for him.

I walked Ms. Alice and Bailey back to Abbey truck when the alarm was pressed and the car blew up right In front of us. We stood there in shock and from the corner of my eye I saw a black SUV speeding off, taking a look at the license plate. I remember the number and will be searching for that damn van. This had Aden and Ron's name all over it and I will be all over their ass.

Bailey

I sat there in the bed stuck, I could not believe my ass would have been blown up with my twins in that truck. Listening to the video of Aden bragging about what he did to me made my stomach turn. Aden working with my father and Mr. Ron was not a good thing at all, he is getting himself in more bullshit with Aaron; then just raping me and fucking up their mother house. I went to visit Farrah a couple times and she is still in a coma that I prayed she gets out of soon, Abbey was on my mind heavy because how she disappeared didn't add up to me one bit.

Abbey told me about the threats her father was sending her, and my guess was that he took her from the school, she was really scared and would always look over her shoulders making sure he was nowhere around. I checked social media like Facebook and shit, and it was dry as fuck, scrolling down my timeline something caught my attention. The conversation Aden and Ron were having had me in deep thought, I wondered who they were talking about and who the hell was this girl they had.

My phone started going off letting me know I had mutual messages and I started to wonder, opening them up pictures started to load and as each one did, I got sick to my stomach. The first couple of pictures was of me when Aden raped me and then the others was Abbey naked her body was buried up and she looked helpless. I dropped my phone screaming loud as tears fell from my eyes. I couldn't believe this was really happening to her again, I wanted to help her out of there so bad but there's only so much I can do now that I'm pregnant.

Aaron and everyone ran in my room asking me questions and I could not even get the words out, I picked up my phone showing everyone what I saw, and they all went from worried to pissed off. Aunt Alice tried to call Abbey's phone back to back, but it would only ring. She tried one last time and the person that answered surprised us all.

"Aye Ms. Alice, how are you doing girl?" Aden spoke

"Where's my daughter?" She asked

"Look she real busy right now but I'll tell her you called" he laughed

"Mom" Abbey yelled

There was this loud smack through the phone, and we all got pissed

"Well look I got to go but I'll tell Abbey you called" he said before hanging up

We all sat there silent for a while and I knew Ron ass had her, we had an idea where she was at now, but we had to play smart. Clever through his phone across the room making us all jump, looking at him I can tell he was more hurt than the rest of us. Even though Abbey would not give him a chance, he cared about her a lot. Ever Since he met her, he liked her and Aaron said it was like love at first sight, he never saw Clever that way.

Looking around I noticed Aunt Alice was gone and the boys began talking, I got up and went out of my room to find her. I heard something towards the kitchen so that is where I headed, I walked in to see my aunt on her knees praying. As the tears spilled from her eyes I began crying too, I got on my knees and joined my aunt in prayer.

Lord, I pray Your emotional, physical, and spiritual protection over my loved ones. Keep evil far from them and help them to trust. You as their refuge and strength. I pray you will guard their minds from harmful instruction and grant them discernment to recognize truth. I pray You will make them strong and courageous in the presence of danger, recognizing that You have overcome and will set right all injustice and wrong one day. Help them to find rest in Your shadow, as they live in the spiritual shelter You provide for them. Let them know that the only safe place is in Jesus, and that their home on earth is only temporary.

"Amen" we said together

We got up, and she began breaking down and I let her cry on my shoulder while rubbing her back. I felt bad for my aunt especially after what Abbey showed me on them papers and most of all we just wanted Abbey back safe and sound. As I thought on, I began breaking down, the tears fell nonstop, and I could not stop them. Aunt Alice began rubbing my back and I continued to cry. I tried to be the strong one inside but deep down I was hurting the most. She was like a sister to me.

"Get up Bailey, Abbey wouldn't want us crying" Aunt Alice said

She helped my big behind and we sat on the coach and began talking. At this point I have no idea where Aaron and them went but I pray they are safe. While my aunt was talking, I zoned out thinking about how both my best friends were in bad shape. Farrah was laying in the hospital in a coma and I am not sure how long she would be in there, but I pray not long. I go talk to her at least two days a week hoping one day she will wake up. I brush her nappy as hair and the doctor told me they ran more tests. I was scared to find out what was going on but listened, Dr. Jones told me that she was now 30 weeks pregnant and her parents did not want anything to with the baby really. Meaning she was pregnant when that truck hit her and my heart broke, Aunt Alice started screaming my name breaking me out of my thoughts.

Looking at her I could see she had been calling me for a while. I apologized and got up off the couch heading to my room. Once I reached it, I laid on the bed rubbing my belly. I needed to relax, there was way too much going on and I cannot be stressing like this. I changed my mind about getting the early DNA Test, the risk was too high, and I did not want my babies to get birth defects. I go get my ultrasound tomorrow and was upset that I had to go without my two best friends. These past months changed so much. I would have never thought that all this shit would have happened, but who I am kidding. We live in this crazy ass world, where no one loves no one. It seems to be that the family did not care for one another anymore, like they had no love for one another.

The twins began kicking the shit out of me and I turned on my side. The pain was getting worse and I could not wait to have my baby's.

The smell of food hit my nose and I admittedly got up following the smell. I walked in the kitchen to see Aunt Alice making my favorite baked ziti. My stomach began growling and I rubbed it, calming the twins down a bit. When they hear Aaron's voice, they start kicking me. My phone began ringing and I picked it up without even looking.

"Hello" I spoke lowly

"Ms. Harrison, did you forget about your doctor's appointment today?" The lady asked over their phone

"Oh shit, I thought it was tomorrow" I blurted out

"No, it was today" she said

"Ok I will be there" I said quickly

"See you soon" she said hanging up

Aunt Alice heard the conversation and started helping me get my life together. I sent Aaron a text about the appointment then finished getting ready. He texted me back saying he will meet me there and Auntie turns off the stove. I waited outside for her and once she came out, we left. We arrived at the doctors and spotted Aaron waiting for us at the door. We found a parking spot and got out at the same time. Once we reached Aaron he spoke, and the kids went crazy. He rubbed my belly and they calmed down, we walked in and I took a seat while Aaron signed us in. The doctor soon came out calling us in and we went in while Aunt Alice waited there. She seemed kind of nervous about something, so she kept looking at her phone. Aaron began shaking me, breaking my thoughts and I did not realize they were talking this whole time. I really wished Abbey and Farrah could be here. I missed them bald headed bitches a lot, I thought laughing to myself Aaron looked back at me.

"Bay what's funny?" Aaron asked me

"Nothing baby shhh the doctor talking" I said listening to her

She asked me to lay down and I did just that. I was 35 weeks pregnant and I had to get two test scans this week since I missed the last one. I was getting a chronicity scan at the same time as a dating scan, one was to see if my babies shared a placenta. I also had to get combined screening for Down's syndrome, which I prayed my babies were safe with. I had to admit I was late as hell getting these tests, so I was scared for my kids and me. After we were there for at least three hours, our babies were in their own placenta and were extremely healthy. I was having a boy and girl, I was over excited. We decided to name them Drew and Dakota, once we reached the waiting area Aunt Alice was gone. We tried calling her but got no answer at all, I prayed she was ok, and we headed home.

I could not wait to get my hands on that damn baked ziti, I need like one big ass plate of it. Aaron was here for me, though there is a chance one of the babies is not his. He still planned to be a great dad to both and I was glad to have him by my side. We made it home and I got out rushing to the house. I had to pee bad as hell and if I did not hurry, I would be a pissy ass. Aaron laughed at me as I rushed to the bathroom and I got a little mad. This was becoming stressful as hell, I got tired of using the bathroom every five minutes.

Chapter 11
Abbey

Being locked up here was the worst and I could not wait to get lost. My father, Aden and Mr. Harrison had talked about me daily and took turns watching me. My father would not let nobody touch me, but his trifling ass did. It felt good to hear my mother's voice and I know it *ticked Aaron off to hear me get hit like that. I sat in my room tied up looking around, I needed to find a way out fast. The door downstairs opened then slammed, it got quiet for a minute. Next thing you know they all start laughing, "pass me that bottle youngblood" my father spoke deeply.*

They have been drinking and I knew my father would soon make his way up here. My body got tense and I hated the feeling, it would be a long time before I am able to give my body to the person I love. My father took away all my happiness and I would not dare let anyone touch me in this way now. The footsteps got closer and louder, I jumped out in fear as the door flew open. My father stood there with the biggest smile ever, he walked over to me and I got scared out of what was going to happen.

My father sat next to me and started rubbing my leg. Moving around I noticed the gun in his back side, he stood up going to the door closing it. He stripped out of his clothes and began walking towards me. I tried to move but my hands were tied up, he climbed on top of me having his way. Shoving himself inside of me repeatedly I cried out in pain, the smile across his face showed he did not care about me. He slowly took the chains off me and made me turn around. He rammed his self-inside of me ass my body started to get weak. Mr. Harrison came in and my father got up letting him have a go. Tears began running down my face as he rammed inside of me, looking over I saw my father watching with a smile.

"your right she is better than her mother" mr Harrison spoke in between breaths

"Told you nigga!! Now get up" my father laughed

For hours they took turns with me and there was not shit I could do at this point. They soon walked out the room only in boxers and I was not chained up anymore. I plan to kill each one of them for what they did to me, Aden raped me without my father permission. I waited so long for them to forget about chaining me up, I started to put my plan in effect before they even noticed. Going to the door I grabbed my father's gun off the floor, sticking it in my purse and I made my way to the bathroom. Turning the scaling hot water on, I let it run down my body. I wanted to wash all their dirty sins off me and I could not believe my father treated my mother this way. I figured that is why he got her put away for all these years. Washing up about 6 times I got out, looking for something to wear. I came across my black sweatpants and a red thermal long sleeve, I opened the door listening to what was going on.

I could hear walking and talking, as the footsteps got closer, I closed the door backing up in the dark. Hearing my father sing for joy made me want to throw up, he was not what you think he was. A crooked cop yes, the best father hell no. I walked out the room heading down the hall to my father's room, opening the door I went in, closing it softly. Listening to him in the shower singing, which only happens when he has a female friend over but no tonight he will not. I opened the bathroom door going in, pulling the shower curtain down and he smiled at me. Backing up some I reached in my purse and started to talk that crazy shit aging.

"Oh, you ready for more, come get in the shower" he said laughing

I pulled out the gun pointing it at him, he looked speechless for a minute. He looked around but could not find what he was looking for, then he looked at me. He turned off the water and began getting out of the shower, I opened the bathroom door and left. I made it to his room, and I could hear his footsteps close behind. Turning around I see him standing by the bathroom door.

"Is that my gun? You little bitch" he asked me

"I don't know!! Is it?" I said back

He charged at me and I pulled the trigger sending two shots to his chest. He fell to the ground and I locked the door, bending over and I looked at him. He began talking barley and it was all lies, he did not love me or care about me. He never saw this coming or thought my big ass had the heart to do it. Mr. Harrison began banging on the door from the noise of the gun going off, and I slid out the window grabbing both phones. Standing in the backyard I pulled out my phone calling Aaron, he picked up and it was quiet. No one said anything so I began talking fast.

"Aaron it's me I need your help, I'm at my father's house. I texted you the address and shit already" I said hanging up

Going through the front door, I hear Mr. Harrison going off. He made his way downstairs and I acted like I did not know what was going on. "Is daddy ok?" I asked he looked up at me and shook his head, he was trying to figure out what the fuck happened. I offered to get him a beer and he agreed to it, going in the kitchen I pulled him out a beer. Since they like it in a cup, I poured it in one, spreading a lot of rat poison in it. I stirred it up. I mixed a little Remy with it and began walking back in the living room. I passed him the cup and watched him begin drinking it.

"I put a little liquor in there, I figured you needed it" I said nicely

"Thank you, Abbey," he said taking a gulp

I pulled out the gun and he looked shocked, getting up I went towards the window. Looking out I see Aden pulling up, I turned back around to Mr. Harrison. "If you say a word, I will kill you" I said walking off into the dark. Aden came in with three women and I thought this was a bad time for this.

"Where's Ron?" He asked

He made his way towards me and I stepped out with the gun pointed at him. He backed up laughing and I am glad he thought this was a joke. He looked over at Mr. Harrison who was now in bad shape and I laughed. I knew for sure Aden had a gun on him, but I wasn't scared to pull the trigger either. Aden always took me as a punk or something because I never fought back against my father.

"Ron dead man" Harrison finally spit out

"This bitch doesn't have the balls!" Aden said laughing

"I got the balls to shoot your dick off right now" I said laughing harder

"Bitch!!" Aden said

He charged at me and we were now fighting over the gun. The door flew open and I just hoped it was Aaron and them, I was not letting him get the gun away from me. He was going to die right here and now, just like the rest of these mother fuckers. The gun went off and everything became a blur.

Aaron

The gun went off and we stood there in shock, I prayed it was not Abbey who got shot. Clever ran over pulling them apart, and Aden's body fell to the ground. Abbey stood there with a bloody side, my guess was they shot each other. Clever was checking on Abbey making sure she was not hurt too badly and I went looking through the house *to make sure there was not any more unexpected guess here. Looking through the first room I saw chains hooked to a bed and the room was a mess. I felt like this where Abbey was held, and my stomach turned. Going down the hall I see a door wide open, pulling out my gun I went straight in. Looking around I see no one, I continued to look around the room when I stepped on something.*

"What the fuck" I yelled out

I looked down to see Mr. Ron laying there dead with his eyes open, I wonder what the hell went on in here. When Abbey called me saying she needed me she was scared, keeping my promises to her I am here but it seems like she did not even need me really. She knew something was up and I bet that is why she called me, Abbey was not a weak girl and knew how to handle stuff on her own. What I could not really understand was why she never really stood up for herself at school or against her father. The window was wide open, and I could hear the sirens getting closer, rushing back to the living room. I told them we had to go now.

We both helped Abbey up and made our way out the door. I knew this guy who was a doctor and could help us with this womb. So, I called him up once we reached the car getting in, the cops pulled up and there were cars everywhere. Going the other way, I looked in my rearview mirror to see them all going in at once, I noticed Abbey in bad pain, and I knew Ms. Alice would not be happy about this at all. We made it back home in about a half hour and the doctor was already there waiting, getting out I went around the back to help with Abbey but Clever had it covered. He had her picked up and I closed the door behind him, going inside I can hear Ms. Alice whimpering.

Bailey has been an emotional wreck since Abbey went missing and I could understand why, she was the only one there for her and Farrah was lying in a coma pregnant. The doctor mentioned that she will never make it out of the coma, but we had hope. Leading the way to Abbey room Clever laid her down on the bed and the doctor asked us to leave. I began walking out when I noticed Clever never moved from her side, I did not say a word, I just left him there and went to check on my baby. I walked in our room to see Bailey laying there balled up crying, she rubbed her belly promising the twins she would give them a better life than what she had.

I got in bed with her and continued to rub her belly, she grabbed my hands pulling me closer. There was something I needed to get off my chest and it seems to be so that she does as well. I wondered how I was going to tell her. I really felt, this pregnancy and the way the shit happened took a toll on me real talk.. I could not believe the way my brother betrayed me, I was always there for him. I wondered where it all went wrong. My brother is now dead, and this will hurt our parents badly, how was I going to even tell them what happened. I knew after the last stunt he pulled with our mother she would not hurt so much, she broke her back to keep his ass out of trouble and all he did was be disrespectful to her.

She turned around staring in my eyes and I did the same, something was really bothering her, and I wanted to know what. Tears were rolling down her face and I wiped them away with my thumb. I could not wait to get them out this fucked up town, and I did not want to raise the twins here. She began talking slowly but I made her stop and take deep breaths first. Looking in her eyes I see her hurt and pain, I prayed we can all move past this shit.

"Aaron, I need to admit something" she said

"What's up baby?" I asked her

"What if one of the babies is Aden?" she asked me

"I will still raise it as my own, even though I don't like the thought of it" I said honestly

"What happened tonight?" she asked looking at me

"When we got there......" I paused for a second

"Aden and Abbey were fighting over guns, the gun went off leaving Clever and I in shock" I said looking down

"Omg Aaron what happened?" she asked getting upset

"They both got shot" I said quietly

The house phone began ringing, Bailey and I looked at each other than to the living room. We got up making our way to it, but it stopped ringing. We made our way to the living room to see Abbey standing there, she had the phone to her ear, and she was saying ok I'm on my way. She looked at us and said we need to get to the hospital now, she said she will explain on the way. We all jumped in my truck and I pulled off, Abbey began telling us what the doctor said but could explain more if we came in. Damn if it was not one thing, it is another this shit was crazy as hell. We pulled up, found a parking spot and got out going in, Abbey looked a little better from how we found her. My phone began ringing and it was Clever, so I stepped to the side picking it up.

Chapter 12
Abbey

The doctor walked into Farrah's room and began talking to us and her parents about her condition. Farrah was having a baby soon in a few weeks and would never be stable enough to take care of it. So, it was *either we take the baby in or the state got it since her parents wanted nothing to do with it and I was not letting that happen. Looking out the door I see this guy walking by, he looked in and kept walking I thought that sit was wierdd as fuck.*

"Look I know it's a process, but I'll take the baby in only if that's ok with her parents" I said bluntly

"I'm fine with that Abbey if you ever need anything let us know, I'm pretty sure that's what she will want" her mother said

"Abbey what she means is we will be here to help throughout the process, we just can't raise another child right now with me getting sick and all" her father spoke kindly

"Abbey there is a process, you need to have a roof over your head and a good job showing that you are able to provide for the baby" the doctor said

Well good thing you just graduated and I can get you a job where I work for a start, I heard about what happened with your father but listen Abbey you have nothing to worry about we all got you" Farrah mother said again

"Seems like you off to a good start with a lot of people here to help Abbey" the doctor said

"yes, and I'm really thankful for them all" I said smiling for the first time

"well she is having a girl and I would like to talk to her mother in my office for a minute" the doctor spoke kindly

"Abbey comes with me" Farrah mother said

"that's fine" she said leading the way

Farrah's mother and I walked with the doctor to her office. There were papers that needed to be signed and with Farrah mothers help I got a little bit of it done. I needed to get a job fast and I had to work on getting a place here until I can get the baby and leave. I did not want to be in this fucked up town no longer than I had too, but I also was not letting my best friend baby go into the system. Bailey has twins on the way so I was not putting that on her either, I am not sure if I'll ever have kids so this will do good. After reading over the paperwork I signed my name and she began talking to me.

"Hey! There was this guy here" she said looking down

"What guy" I asked

"He was trying to smother her, but he claims to be the baby dad" she said

"The baby comes with us until Abbey gets her job and place period because from what I know that man is bad news" Farrah mother said worried

After the doctor had a talk with us, I began walking down the hall with thoughts floating through my head. I could not believe this shit, I really wanted to know who the hell he was. I walked back in the room and told them it was time to go. On our way out I see that guy again, the one who was looking in the room when we first got here. I wondered if he was the one but did not want to go pointing my finger. We made it to the car, and I was still in deep thought, Aaron began screaming my name and it broke me out of my thoughts. Looking up at them, they were staring at me weirdly. I began telling them what she told me, and they got pissed off also.

"Abbey we here for you, little mama will be safe, and she will love you" Bailey spoke softly

"What are you going to name her?" Aaron asked me

"Farrah after her mom" I said

I had to do a lot of shopping for the baby girl. She was going to have anything she wanted, and I will always be there to listen to her. Clever really liked me and he has been by my side since I came back, I was grateful for that honestly. I want to know what he is going to think, when I tell him I am taking on this baby as my own. Once we made it home, Aaron parked, and we all got out heading inside. We went our separate ways and I walked in my room to see Clever waiting for me. I took a seat next to him, I was not comfortable, but I would not push a good man away either. I told him about the baby and what the doctor said, he agreed, rubbing my hand and it made me feel at ease. We talked about the stuff the baby would need, and he agreed to go with Bailey and me. I could not get what the doctor told out my head though, I could not believe this nigga came there trying to kill my bitch. I was going to take good care of her child and make sure she far away from that nigga. Plus, Aaron and Clever would have a fucking fit if anything happens to Bailey, me or the kids.

Next Morning

I woke up to the smell of food and I could not wait to get some of that. I got up going in the bathroom to shower, stopping at the mirror. I see all the scars my father caused me. It made me hate my body and I could not stand to look at it. I let the hot water run down my body and it calms me a little bit. After my thirty minutes shower I got out going back to my room, I threw on a sweat suit and headed to the kitchen. Bailey and my mother sat at the table talking, and I joined them. I *noticed the boys were gone and I wondered what they were up to. We still needed to go shopping for all three kids and I guess my mother was tagging along. My mother never asked about my father or if he was ok and it felt good because no one really understood what I went through with him. We talked and laughed the whole time and it felt good to be back, I have not eaten this good in a while. The feeling of me being a mom made me happy as hell inside and I could not wait even though I was not pushing it out. I wanted to be the mom like I did not have, after we were done eating, we all got up putting our shoes on. Once we were all ready, we headed out the door. I missed driving my bitch Rosie, so we drove in my candy red Ford Focus.*

I turned on the radio to find out it was supposed to snow, and we all hissed under our breaths. I could not believe this shit, why did it not snow on Christmas. Why wait until January to fucking snow, Mother Nature was killing a bitch. We pulled up to the mall and I parked in a spot right in the front. We got out heading inside the mall, I got so excited that I could not wait to go shopping. My mom got a phone call leaving Bailey and I alone, we wandered off into a baby store close by.

Looking around I see a lot of shit I want to buy for all three babies, going to a wreck I picked up a couple outfits. Children's place always has a sale and I am glad to be catching one at a time like this. I really wanted to go to baby r us, but this will do for now, turning around to find Bailey someone bumped into me making me drop everything. Looking up I see the dude from the hospital, he looked at me and said big bitch then walked off. I got up looking around and dude was nowhere in sight, I thought maybe I was losing it until Bailey walked up.

"Abbey, who was that nigga?" she said looking around

"have no clue but I seen him that night at the hospital" I said picking up the stuff

"You think he's the one?" she asked me

"I think so" I agreed

We looked around for a little while longer before paying and leaving out. That shit was just so wired, and dude did not even know me to be calling me a big bitch. Why did this dude keep popping up out of nowhere like this, I wanted to know what connection he had with Farrah? She was telling us what happened but then she went into that coma, I prayed she made it out safe and back to normal. My mother walked up on us making us both jump, she looked at us wired and we just stood there speechless. We walked off and she followed close behind us, we looked around and he was nowhere in sight like he just disappeared. Dude was wired as fuck and I just do not have time for the shit, like I have way too much on my plate right now.

Couple hours later we were done shopping and it was peaceful. I was going to mention this shit to Clever because if anything happens to me, they know who to go to. We made our way out the mall in full blown laughs, unlocking my car Bailey stopped walking. Looking over I see the dude grabbing himself, turning around to see if my mother caught that he was gone. She looked at us wierd again and I could not understand how the fuck her ass kept missing him.

"Girls what's going on?" she asked us

"Mom, are you telling me you didn't just see that?" I asked her

"No baby!! I was in my phone sorry" she said upset

I shook my head looking around while going to my car getting in, I could hear Bailey footsteps close behind me. I wanted to know what he wanted, and why he was at the hospital that night. We could not leave for college until after I got the baby and I could not wait for it to be over with. I just could not wait to leave this fucked up town and I needed to get away from it fast. Once we arrived home, we all got out leaving the bags, I figured the boys would get them out. We went in to hear the boys watching football, Faheem loudmouth echoed out and I wished he shut up. We went into the living room and all eyes were on us, the boys were just staring at us and I just walked away. I did not know if what happened today was showing on my face or not, and I did not waste any time trying to figure it out. Soon I reached my room door Clever grabbed me, turning me around, he smelled so damn good and he looked incredibly good like he just got a shape up. He stared at me with his big brown eyes and it made my heart melt, turned my head looking away and he made me face him again.

"What's going on?" he asked me

"Nothing boo" I said sweetly

"The minute you walked in the living room, we could tell something was up now spill it" he said cocky

"There was this boy following us around and my mother didn't catch neither time" I said going in the room

He followed behind gathering his thoughts and I sat on the bed watching him, he stood there with his hand on his chin looking around.

"Wait you said a boy was following yawl around" he said sitting down

"Yeah, he called me a big bitch, after knocking all my stuff out my hand. Then he grabbed his stuff at Bailey" I said shaking my head

He just sat there listening to me and he did not say a word, when I was done, he just gave me a kiss and walked out. I got up following close behind him and he was gone, I knew for a fact he was mad and looking at Bailey I could see Aaron was out too. My mother made us some popcorn and we sat there looking for a movie, praying the boys do not get into trouble out there. My mother was quiet the whole time and I guess after hearing what happened she felt bad, I did not want her to feel bad about it. I know she had to live her life too because it is obvious, she did not get too with dad. I called my mother over, so she can sit with us and she began smiling from ear to ear, we were glad to have her here now and she was the bomb didn't even look her age at all. My mother stood 5'6 with light brown eyes and wavy hair, she was thick as hell and had deep dimples. Medea Halloween 2 came on and we began watching it, this movie was funny as fuck. She be fucking them clowns up, and I do not blame her. We watched a couple more movies and hours passed, the boys still have not showed back up and I began to worry kind of.

Chapter 13
Bailey

This shit was crazy, and that nigga was even crazier, why the fuck was he following us around? When Farrah said she got wrapped up with bad people, I had no idea they were this bad. Apparently, Aaron and Clever know who dude is, something about a run in at a club while back. Faheem just sat there quiet and I knew for sure shit got real, we have not seen them since that day, and I prayed everything will be ok. My due date was slowly approaching, and I had to prepare for these results. I was going to be the best mom to my twins, and I was going to finish college. I was glad that Abbey was going to take care of

Farrah baby and she finally had something to be happy about. As I thought about it, I wondered, was he the baby dad, the guy she got wrapped up with.

Dude was playing it too close and I just was not beat, especially since I am pregnant with twins and would not be able to do a damn thing. The doorbell rang and it broke my thoughts. I opened the door to see no one there. Looking around I did not see any cars or anything around, getting ready to shut the door I saw this envelope. I picked it up and closed the door, locking it. I made my way back to the living room to see Abbey sitting there. This envelope was thick as hell and I wondered, opening it up I would see pictures of Farrah. I got Abbey's attention and began showing her pictures, as we got deeper in the pictures. There were pictures of Abbey and I in the shower, there were pictures of Aunt Alice and her lover.

"Dude playing a dangerous game" Abbey stated

"He has to be the one Farrah was talking about" I said sitting the photos down

"Little mama is not going with him" she said shaking her head

"Hell no, he will do her like he did Farrah" I stated

"We are leaving after we get the baby?" She asked me

"That's what Aaron said" I said sitting back

We sat and talked a little more, even though we both were weirded out about those pictures. We tried not to let it get to us. I wanted to know what his purpose is, did he not do enough to Farrah already. I needed to know the whole run-down story because something is missing from my point of view.

Abbey

This shit was getting crazy and getting out of hand now, I been through enough I was not about to let this nigga come and snatch my little bit of joy. How did he even get all these damn pictures of us, he must be watching us or something? I wondered what happened at the club that night, I know he was cool with Aden but smash that, that nigga dead no heart feelings. We have not seen the boys in a week, and I did not like hearing from them. Looking over, Bailey started having pains, she grabbed her belly as she cried out. I was stuck on what to do but then I realized she was about to give birth. Screaming for my mother she came running in, she looked at us and noticed what was going on.

"Oh, shit damn fuck" she said running off

I held her hand and sent Aaron a text with the other, my mother came running in again and we helped her up. Soon she stood to her feet, her water breaking splashing all over the floor. We rushed her to the car and I sped off once everyone was in, doing 90 all the way there we made it in no time. I pulled up in the first place I saw and jumped out, looking to my right I saw the boys. I ran inside to get the nurses and shit because my bitch was in pain, they all ran out at once and she got put on that bed shit. They rushed her in, and we waited, Aaron went back with her and I told him to take lots of pics. We sat there in silence and Clever grabbed my hand. I wanted to snatch it away but then I needed him, and I missed him most of all. Clever became someone I can talk to besides Aaron, I can tell he really loved and cared about me. The day they found me and brought me home, he had not really left my side. He was always one step behind me, if he's not beside me. It felt good to have someone who cares for me, not to mention he understands that I am not ready.

We talked and held hands while my mother talked on the phone. She did that a lot lately and I wanted to meet her new boo thang. The doctor came out calling my name, Clever and I got up to see if everything was ok. The look on her face made me uneasy, and I kind of did not want to know what she was about to say.

"Hi Abbey! It's nice to see you again but I have good and bad news for you" she said smiling

"I'll take the good first" I said

"Your little girl is here, and she is healthy, but we need to run test because she is a little early" she said

"Can we see her" Clever asked

"Sure, right this way" she said leading the way

She led the way and we followed close behind her. I was happy to finally have baby girl and I was scared to find out the bad news. When Farrah makes it out of that coma, she is going to be happy that I did such a good job. We walked into the nursery and she handed us our daughter. She looked like Farrah in every way, and it brought a big smile to my face. I let Clever hold her while I go talk to her in the Hallway.

"Hey Abbey! It is time I tell you the bad news" she looked at me upset

"Ok" I said looking away

"Farrah is gone, she passed away this morning. That guy came back and one of the new nurses let him in, not knowing the situation. I'm really sorry" she said in one breath

I just stood there because I had no words, I could not believe what I was hearing. It made sense why she was here so early. I was glad the baby was healthy but upset that Farrah was gone. The tears began to fall and there was no stopping them, when her words finally hit me, I broke down crying. This couldn't be true, and I must be dreaming. I fell to the ground hitting it hard because I couldn't believe what I was hearing. I prayed she made it out of that coma, and I wondered why God did not answer my prayers this time.

Clever came running out and I cried into his chest, I know I was taught by Bailey mom that everything happens for a reason and God makes no mistakes. This was really taking a toll on me, we had so many plans and she would not be here with us to see them through. How will I explain this to her daughter when she is old enough to understand, I will never be the parent to lie to her child. I will be her best friend but also, the mother she respects.

Clever helped me up and dried my face, he looked deep in my eyes and I could tell he felt my pain. I hugged him tight and thought about how Farrah would have been cursing me out if she saw my ass crying. We got to bring her home in a couple days and I was excited to leave this town. I knew I had to get the rest of the stuff in her nursery tonight because that lady comes tomorrow to see if capable of having her. In which I have everything she is going to need set up already. I did not want to raise Kelsie here and I would not dare, there were so many bad vibes here that I just needed a greasy start. Going off to college was my dream and just because I now had a child to fend for does not mean I was giving that up.

"Abbey I'm really sorry for your loss, my husband just texted me and said your cousin had the twins. We can take her and go up there if you want" *she spoke softly*

"Yes, thank you and also thank you for being honest with us and begin a friend" I said hugging her

She hugged me back and Clever went to get the baby. Once he came back out, we made our way to go see the twins. Farrah's parents showed up and I went to show them little mama before I went to see Bailey. They held her and I saw tears fall from their eyes Dr. Jones mentioned she needed to talk to them, and they handed her back, giving me a kiss on the forehead saying I am such a blessing. I told them we'll see them real soon and we made our way to see Bailey once we reached the room. I can see how happy Bailey and Aaron were, it brings a big smile to my face. We went in joining them and we were all happy for once, they held Farrah while we played with the twin. They favored both and had the deepest dimples, they looked just alike and you sure would get them mixed up if one was not a girl.

"So, we got the results back in like 2 days and I prayed Aden is not one of the twin's father" she said looking down

"Look baby I already told you, I don't care I'm here for you" Aaron said kissing her

"Awe yall so cute" Clever teased

"Abbey what's wrong, why are you so quiet?" Bailey asked me

"I don't want to mess up the good mood" I said playing with the baby

"Tell me please" She begged

"Farrah passed away" I said in a hurry

"Yeah doctor jones told us that oh boy came back and did something to her. So, they had to take the baby out, right away" Clever added

They sat there shocked and I am quite sure that is how I looked when Dr. Jones told me. Bailey began crying and I broke down too, who would have thought this would happen, we never in our lives imagined this. The babies began crying and the boys had a rough time trying to calm them down. I got Farrah and began rocking her. She calmed down some, she looked into my eyes and smiled at me.

It made me feel good inside, she liked me already and I was glad to say she was my baby and have a part of Farrah still with us. Once she fell asleep, I gave her back to Clever and he watched him amazed. He kissed her forehead and whispered to her how he will always be one call away. I got up going to the bed to sit with my cousin, she scooted over, and we laid there. I knew my ass should not be in this bed, but we made it work, Aaron and Clever laughed at us taking pictures and we posed for the camera. This will be a day we will never, be able to forget, the boys went to get food and we sat and talked. Farrah passing away just did not sit right with us, and how did he even get past that dumb ass nurse. I wanted to kill him myself, I saw a picture of him, and he was the man following us around. He pushed it way too far and he will get what he is barring for it.

Chapter 14
2 days later
Abbey

Today was the day we got to take our babies home; I have not gone home or left Farrah since I got her. When the lady came with her she was impressed, she mentioned to me how I do have full custody of her after I sign the papers which I was with because we were moving soon and Farrah parents agreed it was best. I have not left this room and I stayed with Bailey the whole time, Bailey just went into the bathroom when Drew started crying. Farrah was sound asleep, so I went over and picked him up, the twins favorite Aaron so much that I did not see Aden in either one of them. Rocking him he looked up at me and I smiled down at him, before I knew it, he was sound asleep.

Bailey came out smiling and I laid Drew back down, my bitch looked good in that outfit. We began packing the kids up while waiting for the doctor to come back with the papers. I got the feeling someone had been watching me and began looking around, I walked to the door looking out to see no one there at all. I hoped my mind was not playing tricks on me, that shit that happened with my father really fucked me up. I will kill anyone who even looks at Farrah that way, it was disgusting, and I could not see how people took pride in doing that. Once everything was packed, we got the kids set up in their car seats. Clever and Aaron walked in with the nurse, then got the car seats while I grabbed some bags. Bailey must get it in the wheelchair out, we got our papers and were gone out of that place. Since we would not be here Aaron will get the birth certificates and send them to us.

Clever and Aaron already bought the houses and said once we land someone will be waiting for us. I was not too comfortable with that, but Faheem will be with us so that eases me. We reached outside and the boys packed the cars up, they brought both cars around and we loaded up. Farrah started crying and I gave her a bottle calming her down, after she was done, I burped her, and she was off to sleep. Strapping her back into the car seat she was sound asleep again, Clever began driving again he looked at me through the rear-view mirror making me smile. I began to wonder, where the hell my mom has been. I have not seen her since the day we brought Bailey in, I know she has a man but damn mom the dick cannot be that good. We pulled up to the house and I saw my mother standing there with this tall guy.

She was smiling hard and the boys just got out grabbing the bags, I watched them give the guy dap before going in. My guess was they knew him, the way he dressed was like he plays ball or some shit. Clever began calling my name, breaking every train of thought I had. Looking over at him, he stood there like he had been calling me for a while.

"Baby you ok? He asked me

"Yes, why?" I questioned back

"Bay I been calling for like 5 minutes now" he spoke concerned

"I'm fine bay but who that guy" I asked him

"That's mom boyfriend Sam, we met him when looking for the houses in Florida" he said helping me out

"Ummm Oh Ok" I said walking towards the house

Once we all were inside the babies were now awoken, and we all sat in the living room talking. Sam was a cool dude, and I can tell he liked my mom a lot. He was a real estate man and played basketball sometimes, but he is retired. I can tell my mother was not used to it and she looked a little uncomfortable, Farrah began crying and I picked her up heading to the kitchen. Clever came into the kitchen not too long after I did and began helping me. He was always there by my side without me even asking him, I never thought I would ever find someone as sweet as him. Unlike everyone else he never picked on my weight or anything, it has been plenty of times that he said he loved me just the way I am. At first, I did not understand because no one ever looked at me that way and I always got picked on.

My father used to tell me that I will never find love, and it hurts most because I knew he did not love me at all. Growing up he will tell me all kinds of bad things, but it did not stop me from loving who I was. I did not need boys following me around because to me it meant your self-esteem was low. I knew who I was and what I wanted to be, for a while I believed every bad thing my father told me was true. The damn ratchet ass kids made my days worse every day adding more drama to my plate, as I began to tear up my mother walked in.

"What's wrong baby girl?" She asked me wiping the tears away

"Mom I just can't believe I have someone like Clever, dad made me feel like I will never find love, or no one will ever care for me" I said honestly

"Look baby girl!! Your father did me and my sister the same way. We lost all self-esteem and thought he was right, I was locked up in that damn place he put me in when she passed away. Your father was an evil man and his own family didn't fuck with him" she said getting sad

"Mom look don't cry, you have a man that really cares for you now. I can see it in the way he looks at you, Mom he really likes you unlike dad did" I said smiling at her

"Your right baby, now let's go before they start wondering" she laughed getting up

Farrah was now asleep and took her to her dad, she began moving around and he rocked her singing a song. She calmed down quickly and was fast asleep, he laid her in the playpen next to the twins. I loved the way Clever and Aaron both interacted with the kids. I knew for sure these kids were in safe hands because they both did not play when it came to family.

Couple days later
Bailey

Our stuff was already down in Florida and we will be on our way there today. I got this feeling someone was watching us and sure enough that dude stood across from us. I told Abbey to look and he just smiled at us disappearing in the crowd. Dude was weird as hell and he damn sure was not getting Farrah, we packed the kids up fast and headed out. I told Aaron and they were here in less than 2 minutes, they helped us get in and we were out. They took us straight to the airport and waited with us. I have not seen Faheem in a while, so I hope he shows up. Aunt Alice soon arrived grabbing one of the baby's. This was a 2 hour and 53-minute flight, so I prayed they would sleep through it. Our plane soon arrived, we boarded, I got upset because Aaron was not coming right now but I pray he stays safe.

2 hours later

We landed and this place was beautiful, we got off the plane and there was someone there waiting for us. He helped us get everything into the truck and we were on our way. It was about 70 degrees here and I got hot fast as hell, Drew started moving around and soon woke up. We pulled up to these houses and they were big from what I am used to, the driver gave us both keys and pointed to the houses that sat next to each other. I walked in my house amazed that Aaron did listen to me, the House was exactly how I said I wanted it. I laid Drew down in the swing and began walking around, the kitchen I fell in love with. It had two stoves and the fridge was big as hell with the ice machine. I jumped up and down for joy and I was happy to be starting my life over. The twins were sleeping in the swings, so I took this time to read a book on kindle, an hour went by and I was finishing the book and that shit was good as hell. I got up and went into the kitchen to make bottles so they could be ready, there was a knock on the door, and I went to get it. Opening the door, I see Abbey and Farrah standing there, they came in and we sat in the living room talking.

It felt so good not to have to keep looking over your shoulder, I can tell Abbey was happy to start over but also upset Clever was not here. She liked him more then she will ever admit but he knows it and is by her side 109%. We were not used to getting treated the way the boys treat us, but it was a damn good feeling. We got in a deep conversation when the doorbell rang, who the hell could it be now I thought out loud. We made our way to the door, we looked at each other before opening it. Once we opened the door, we could not believe our eyes and I wanted to know if this was a dream. Faheem stood there with this little boy who looked just like him, he was about 2 and a half years old and he had every feature as Faheem. He pushed past us going straight to the living room, he sat down and the little was not too far away.

"I'm glad to finally see the kids" he said smiling at us

"What's going on Faheem?" Abbey asked

"I came here 2 year ago for college tour, I met this cute as girl and we ended up fucking. I recently found out that she had my child, shorty was not going to tell me either. When Clever, Aaron and I came here to buy the houses, I ran into her and she had Jase with her looking just like me." Faheem said shaking his head

"Well damn bro" we both said

"What's been up with yall" he asked changing the subject

"You heard about that dude, right?" I asked him

"What dude" he asked confused

"Someone been stalking us, I'm glad we moved but I hope he wasn't watching or anything like that" I said honestly

"Dude was really creepy, he even sent pictures to our house in Trenton" Abbey added in

Faheem sat there speechless and junior went to see the babies ima call little man junior cause he spitting imagine of Faheem, I thought Aaron told him. We did not keep nothing from Faheem, he was like a brother we never had. Time sure as hell flew by and it was now dark outside, my tummy began to growl, and I decided to just make something quick to eat. Jase was knocked out on the sofa and we all went into the kitchen. My phone began ringing and I saw my bay name show up, answering his call. I put it on speaker.

"Hey baby what's up" he said through the phone

"Nothing much sitting with Abbey and Faheem" I said looking for something to make

"Hey bro" they both spoke

"What's up y'all" he said back laughing

"Did you know he had a kid?" Abbey asked

"Yeah I did" he said honestly

We talked to Aaron and Clever a little while longer since we will not see them for at least 3 months but at least we had Faheem. The food was almost done, and I was happy as hell. I made some fried chicken, once it was done, we all made a plate and went to watch tv. Jase soon woke up and wanted chicken too, so he ate off everyone's plate. We watched Cars 2 and he was happy as hell. I see Faheem enjoyed being a dad and it made him smile to see his son happy.

They left a while after because of a phone call, it sounded like his baby mom and he was pissed. I wondered who this girl was and what her problem was. Abbey and I watched a movie for a while before she drifted off to sleep on me. I stayed up a little while longer just thinking but my eyes soon got heavy and I drifted off to sleep. I woke up to the sound of babies crying and Abbey gone, I got up stretching heading for the kitchen. I walked in to see Abbey making bottles, I helped her, and we went back to the living room feeding the babies.

Faheem

Tina ass had me fucked up if she thought I was going to let her treat my child any type of way, Naw my momma did not raise me that way. Soon as I pulled up outside of her house Jase started crying, looking back I wondered what was wrong with him. The look on his face told me he did not want to be here, pulling out my phone I told her I am keeping him overnight. Pulling off I headed home, and Jase soon stopped crying and I will figure this out when I get there because something was not right at all.

Once I made it home, we got out heading inside, making sure I locked up and we headed to the living room. I turned on cars 2 and want to grab some snacks for us, I was going to protect my son at any means fuck what his mom had to say. I was not a deadbeat dad and never will be, I was raised right I don't know about these other niggas, but Tina had me fucked up if she thought any different. Grabbing all the snacks I headed back to the living room sitting everything down I asked Jase what was wrong.

"why was you crying when I was about to drop you off home" I asked him concerned

"I don't want to be there anymore daddy" he said looking down

"why what happened?" I asked him really concerned now

"one night I was crying for you and mommy had company, they got mad because I kept crying and she let him beat me" he said starting to cry

I did not even need to hear anything else he was not going back there, I told him it was bath time then after that bedtime and he wiped his tears away. I went to run his bath water while he got ready. Once it was warm, I called for him and he came running in with his towel and rag. When he got undressed, I noticed the marks on his body and I got pissed off, for one he is only 2 years old. Like how can you let someone do that to your child. My mind was really made up now he was not going back there, and I will be getting full custody of my son asap.

After I got him cleaned up and in bed, I headed to the living room to make some calls. Tina was really on some other shit letting another nigga hit my child like I am not around or something. She could have picked up the phone and called me. I would've picked him up, the more I thought about it I got pissed off. Laying down across the sofa I pulled out my phone calling my boy Sam, I knew for a fact he will be able to help me with this court shit. I would have asked Abbey and Bailey, but they have a lot going on themselves so I am not about to add on to that even though I know they would not mind helping me. Once he answered the phone, I started telling him everything, this shit with Tina was really weighing on me heavy like she a fucked-up person and I wish I would have known that before I smashed.

This loud bang was at my door and I jumped up grabbing my strap from under sofa, looking up the steps to make sure my little man did not wake up I made my way to the door. Looking out I see Tina standing there looking mad as hell, but I could not figure out why the fuck is she at my house. I opened the door with my bitch out and she jumped back a little, she looked a mess her hair was all over the place and she was dressed like she just left someone strip club. She began talking and I do not really give a fuck because she not getting my son.

"Faheem where is my son" she asked looking pissed as hell

"Man go head he not coming back there, he is staying with me I seen all them marks on my son and he told me what happened" I said pissed off

"he lien to you" she cried out

"Bitch, you know what get away from my door I'll see you in court" I said closing the door

I had to close the door on her because she was making me want to choke her ass, heading upstairs I went to check on my little man before going to lay down. My mind was all over the place and I needed to relax before I did something I will regret later.

Chapter 15
Aaron 3 months later

I got a call, and I was told that my brother was in a coma. I wondered what the chances were, but I needed to get to my family. Clever and I got off the plane in Florida jumping in his all black Audi, speeding off we headed home. We arrived and went our separate ways, I walked into the smell of steak yellow rice and mac & cheese. I made my way towards the kitchen when I heard the twins, I went into the living to see them getting fussy.

I picked them up kissing them, I honestly missed my babies, and I could not wait to get back to them. I made my way to the kitchen and caught Bailey by surprise, she was smiling from ear to ear and I just knew I had a keeper. She grabbed one of the twins and we sat at the table talking while feeding the kids. Their first day of college started soon and they were happy as hell. These three months away killed nigga honestly, I missed the shit out of them.

I was glad to see them accomplish this goal and I was proud they were following their own dream not someone else's. Clever decided on taking classes online because Kelsie and Abbey did not like it at first, but someone had to be home with her. Clever did not want to stop Abbey from following her dream, and plus the boy only needed a couple more credits to get his degree. It honestly felt good to be back on a positive path, but I also knew my father would not let it last that long.

I did not know how people choose the streets every time, I have learned my lesson and had my fair share. I wanted out of that shit and it's why we moved, the twins were soon asleep so we laid them down. There was a quick knock on the door before it flew open, and I just knew it was Abbey ass. She looked a little upset and I wondered what was wrong, Clever followed close behind her and he looked pissed. I told him let's go chat it up out front and we made our way out the door.

Clever and I met when we were young, his parents just moved him from Florida. He knew this area very well and from what he told me things were not always good. I wondered what the hell happened though, I sat on the brick wall and pulled out a blunt. I lit it and began taking pulls, he paced back and forth, and the shit was getting annoying as hell.

"What's up bro?" I asked

"Remember I told you about the girl I fell in love with?" He asked me

"The one who slept with your dad right?" I asked

"Yeah her Rena, the bitch had the nerve to call my phone and how she got the number I don't fucking know" he said sitting down

"Abbey heard the conversation?" I asked

"She picked up the phone, look bro you know how I feel about Abbey and I don't want to mess this up with her" he said honestly

"Tell her the truth, she is very understanding trust me" I said passing him the blunt

We sat and talked while smoking, my boy was really hurt, and I guess just the thought of losing Abbey made him mad. I do not know who this girl is but she better get lost, that bitch had to do some real digging to find his number. Bailey soon came out and joined us and she seemed upset too, she began talking so we shut up fast.

"Clever I don't know who this girl, but she better gets back" she said a little angry

"I don't know how she got my number honestly" clever spoke

"Abbey is really hurt by this, but she believes you" Bailey said taking a pull of the blunt

"I would never do anything like that to her, I care about her way too much to just let her go. I actually love her!" He said shaking his head

"I'm heading home tell Abbey her and Kelsie can come home" he said walking off

Why did this bitch want to pop up all of a sudden? When she broke the boy's heart; when she slept with his pops. That was real fucked up and deep as hell, I wish a bitch would, I would hurt the both of them on everything I love. Abbey soon came out with Kelsie looking sleepy as hell, I grabbed little mama and walked her home. I began telling her how he really felt about her and what really went down with that girl, she got pissed as hell and grabbed little mama going in. I knew she was not mad at me but at the fact that it happened, Clever was sweet on the inside and would give the last dime in his pocket. I went back home and climbed into bed with my baby. I hope everything works out for the better and I knew for sure they were not letting go without putting up a fight.

2 Days Later
Abbey

I ran around the room looking for something to wear. Today was my first day of college and I was happy as hell to get my career started. Clever and Kelsie were already dressed, and I was still looking for something to wear. I came across my black skinny legs and a white polo shirt, throwing on my black and white Adidas. I headed out. We all left out and headed to the college, most likely I will have to wear a uniform, but I am cool with that also. We pulled and Clever got out, opening my door, I kissed him and met up with Bailey at the entrance.

We bumped into Faheem and he showed us to the main office, we got our classes and headed to the first period. We both were going to be a doctor's and open our own hospital practice one day, we walked into the class and everyone was all around. We took a seat and began listening to the teacher. I began writing down notes and so I will not miss anything when a test comes. Class was over and we headed out when this group of girls bumped into me, what the hell is their problem?

"Umm excuse me you got a problem?" I asked her

"Yeah bitch I do" she said pissed

It made me laugh because I did not care about her ass being mad, for one I did not do shit to the bitch and for two I was done letting people run over me. I just stood there looking at her and she got madder, but I really wanted to know what her problem was.

"What is it sweetheart" I spoke kindly

"You stole my man" she rolled her eyes

"What man bitch" I said getting mad

"Clever hoe" she said getting mad

"Oh, you the hoe who called his phone, look I'll be really nice about this stay away from him or you will see me. Oh, and he don't want your ass, stay outta people's dad's bed before you step to me" I said walking away

Bailey and I made our way through the school, I really did not have time for the bitch. I moved here to start over, but I guess I will forever have to show a bitch I am not the one. This girl really had me fucked up, I know how she crushed him, and I was not letting her come back to steal his joy. The next couple of hours we sat through classes, writing down notes and this girl was really giving me dirty looks. It was the last class, and I could not wait to go home and see my family. I missed them a lot, but I had a dream to chase and to make sure we were good.

Clever met me outside and gave me a kiss, we jumped in the truck and headed home. That girl was really pissing me off, I am quite sure it showed all over my face. I was not paying attention to anything Clever was telling me, I just wanted to strangle her ass. We made it home and I grabbed my bag. I had mad homework but first I wanted to play with babygirl. We all went inside and sat in the living room. I got Kelsie out of her car seat and began playing with her. Clever began asking me how my day was and I thought about that nappy head bitch.

"How was class bay" he smiled at me

"I met that girl, she annoying as hell" I rolled my eyes

"She didn't touch you right?" He asked concerned

"Hell, no or you would've been picking me up from the county jail" I said honestly

"That's my baby" he said kissing me

He got Kelsie to sleep and I pulled out my books, I had a lot of homework and clearly was behind in a lot of shit. Clever sat and helped me with my homework and I am surprised he knew this shit, he even cooked us dinner. He made my favorite baked ziti and I jumped for joy, he warmed up my plate and I finished up my homework. He arrived back with my plate and orange soda, we ate and watched a movie together. He really made me happy and I see I did the same for *him, there was no way I would ever give up this relationship without a fight. He was my first love. I had to admit it.*

I woke up to the sound of Kelsie crying, I looked at the time and it was 6am. I picked her up making my way to the kitchen, I sat her in the swing and began getting her bottle together. She began crying again and I picked her up checking her pamper, she was wet, so I went to change her. Once I was done, I put her back in the swing, then went to grab her bottle. I fed her and she got quiet looking up at me, all she did was sleep, eat and use the bathroom.

I laid on the couch with Kelsie on my chest just thinking, I needed to protect her from all the bad people who hid in plain sight. My father really traumatized me, he did all the things I never thought he would. Looking down at Kelsie she was fast asleep, she reminded me so much of Farrah and I loved having a piece of her with me. When she gets old enough, I will tell her about her mother and anything she wanted to know.

I pulled out my phone texting Bailey, I wondered what she and the twins were doing. It was now 7:30am and I needed to get ready for class, Clever was pissed when I told him about the girl. I really could not believe she slept with his father, that is nasty as hell like his dick all old and shit. "Bitches Crazy" I thought out loud, I laid Kelsie down next to Clever and began getting dressed.

They were laying the same way and I had to take a picture, texting Bailey back I told her meet me outside I am driving. I was not going to bother Clever this morning, he looked so peaceful. Once I was fully dressed, I ran around getting everything I needed, making sure I had all my work. I kissed them goodbye before leaving out. I walked out making it to the car just as Abbey was, we jumped in heading to class. I was not in the mood for that girl today, so if she does not want to be smacked, she better let me be.

Chapter 16
Clever

I woke up going to the bathroom, my phone started ringing off the hook and It made Kelsie wake up crying. Whoever this is better have a good reason why they are calling so much, once I was done, I washed my hands making my way to the baby. She was the most adorable little girl, I couldn't wait for Abbey and me to make our own. Picking her up she smiled at me and got calm, I tried feeding her, but she did not want it and she was wet.

She has me wrapped around her finger already, I hated to see her or Abbey cry and would do anything to keep them smiling. Kelsie wanted me to hold her and I did just that until she slowly drifted back to sleep. My phone began ringing again, I laid Kelsie in her swing and went to get the phone. I made it to my room looking at the missed calls, Rena was really pissing me off and I do not want shit to do with her. I advise her to stop fucking with Abbey because my baby crazy she do not got it all.

I made my way back to the living room taking a seat, and multiple messages came in from her. She was mad Abbey drove my car, she was mad because we got Farrah and I do not want her ass. Putting the bitch on the block I kicked my feet up watching tv, my foot door opened and then closed.

"What the hell is going on here?" I thought to myself

I heard talking and knew who it was right away, Faheem and Aaron came in with the twins. Faheem did not look too happy, my bro looked stressed as hell. His baby mom was a bitch word for life, no matter what Faheem did she made a problem out of it. We sat talking for a while. The babies were asleep and Jase was playing with cars.

"She got me kicked out of college" Faheem spoke pissed

"What the fuck when?" Aaron asked mad

"What the fuck happened?" I chipped in

"The bitch mad because I don't like her in that way, she got niggas in and out of her house daily, so I don't understand. Jase told me one of them hit him, I did a 360 full body check and my boy had a bruise on his back. I asked her and she said he was lying, I showed it to her and she did not have shit to say but he was acting out crying for me. I told her I was getting full custody of him, so her and her best friend Rena did some shit and I got kicked out" he said pissed off getting up

Before we could even say anything else, my phone started to ring off the hook again. This unknown number popped up and I sent it to voicemail, I do not know who the fuck that was calling me. It called a couple more times and I decided to answer it by putting it on speaker.

"Hello" I said husky

"You have a collect call from Abbey, do you wish to accept these charges" the operator went on and on

"Yes" I said as we all sat there confused

I thought she was in school so how the hell, she ended up in jail. Then it fucking it hit me Rena ass and all the texts she sent me. I could not believe my baby was in jail and what the hell happened. Where the fuck was Bailey at, but I only knew she was in jail right along with Abbey. My thoughts were broken when Abbey began talking, she sounded fed up with everything and I needed my baby out of there ASAP.

"Bay" she said softly

"yeah" I said trying not to scream at her

"Your mad right and I bet Aaron is there too" she said again

"Oh, and don't forget me I'm here too" Faheem said even madder

"I can explain" she said quiet

"Spill it" Aaron said

"Don't leave nothing out either" I added in

"We pulled up to the college and parked, we were making our way inside. We hear this talking about Faheem and how he was a deadbeat father. Looking back we notice your ex and some nappy headed hoe. Brushing it off we began walking towards the school again when something smashed the car." She said mad

"Rena and his baby mom Tina" I said pissed as hell

"Well our bail is a lot of money and I don't mind sitting my time in" she said quickly

"Oh, hell no!!! Y'all getting out of there" I said again

"Please stop touching her" she said

"If yall don't sit yall ass down looking like two gay men"

"Bitch I will"

Was the last thing she said before the phone hung up, we all sat there stuck as hell. What the fuck was we going to do, I picked up my phone calling her mom. I explained everything to her, and she was on her way. This shit was really taking a toll on me, we needed to get them out of there ASAP. Momma Alice finally showed up and told us what she found out, long story short they cannot see a judge until Monday since today Friday.

The thought of them sitting there over the weekend bugged the shit out of me, then Kelsie will be missing her also. Rena and Tina got what they deserved, they had no right doing what they did. I was really pissed the fuck off, I want to strangle the bitch myself. Rena knew what the fuck she was doing, the bitch wanted her to get in trouble and kicked out. Rena and Tina were really messing with the wrong people, they did not give a shit about anything, especially Abbey.

Faheem

I pulled up to the park to meet up with my boy Sam, Junior and I got out and he ran off to the park. I smiled at him because he was happy for a chance, I really hated the way Tina treated my boy. She did anything those niggas told her to do and she went too far letting a nigga hit my kid. Sam and I began talking while our kids played and my boy was speaking some real shit. I told him everything that has been going on and he was pissed as hell also, he told me about his sister working at the Women's Detention Center. Sam told me that he will have his little sister look into it, we talked about everything else. Aaron was pissed I got kicked out of college and I never wanted to disappoint him. I will do everything I can to graduate, I refuse to turn to the streets like my father did.

My phone began ringing and I pulled it out looking at the screen, Tina ass was calling me back to back and I really wanted to know why. Junior told me he did not want to go back, and he had my word I was not taking him back. Sam sat there shaking his head already knowing what the hell was going on, this bitch was really getting under my skin. What I could not understand was how can you put a nigga needs before your kid, I would never be in a relationship with her trifling ass. She kept calling so I decided to answer and see what the bitch wanted.

"What do you want?" I said annoyed

"Where is my son" She asked

"He is playing right now" I said watching him run around

"Can I at least speak with him" she questioned

"Junior" I yelled

He came running over with a big smile and I hated to fuck up his mood right now.

"Yea dad" he said once he reached me

"Hey baby!! Mommy miss you" Tina said

"Hey mom" he said dry as hell making Sam and I laugh

"What's wrong baby" she said upset a little

"Junior" she said again

"Well when you are coming back home?" She asked him

"Stay with daddy" he finally said

She got quiet before the phone hung up, Tina just hung up the fucking phone on our son. That bitch was crazy and had me fucked up, he was not going back there I gave my word, and I was going to keep it. Junior had everything he needed at my house, so I did not need anything from her. Junior went back to play, and we smoked a blunt talking.

It began getting dark, so we headed back to Clever house, I knew Aaron was probably over there with the boys anyway. It was taking a toll on us all with the girls being gone, they were a big part of this family. I pulled up to the house and we got out, Abbey Mom was still here so I just knew she cooked. Junior looked at her as a grandma and that was cool with me, he ran straight in the house heading for the babies.

He loved these babies a lot and would sit with them for hours watching over them. He was only 1 years old, but he was smart as hell, his words were clear enough for you to understand most things he said. Momma Alice and Junior went into the kitchen, I sat back watching them play Madden. I was up next and could not wait to get beat by their ass in this game. I wondered if I had spoken to the girls today.

Chapter 17
Abbey

I missed my family so much, I just wanted to hold my baby girl. I had the worst temper ever and what my father did to me made me snap easily. I could have killed that girl in the parking lot, and I sure would snap that man looking bitch neck too. People have been trying us since we got here, and we must sit here all weekend. I could catch a charge fucking with these dumb bitches and I just was trying to chill. I was not going to let a bitch bully us though and when I swung Bailey followed up.

Talking to Clever hearing how upset he was scared me badly, this girl came over snatching my things and spit on me. All I saw was red and before I knew it, I was beating that ass, all the guards came running in pulling us apart. I got put in the hole and it was cold ass shit in here, I sat on the hard mattress with my knees to my chest. What did I become because I was never this reckless, now was the time to admit my father's actions took a big toll on me.

The worst part of being in this damn place was that nasty ass guard, he looked at Bailey and I like we were two new pieces of candy that just came out. It made me feel nasty just like my father did, I began hearing keys jiggling around. The door came open and his big ass stood there licking his lips, he came closer to me and I jumped up in fear. His voice was very husky and deep, the scar above his lip and his built body made me scared as hell. He was troubled and I can feel it, the feeling of what was about to happen was way too familiar.

"Abbey you know I like it when girls make it in here" he said

"Please don't touch me" I said lowly

"Ha!! Your funny all I know is no one better find out about this" he said

He turned me around pulling down my pants and I tried to fight him off, he smacked me across the face and rammed his dick inside of my ass. I could not believe this was happening to me again and by a dam another Crooked ass cop. This showed no matter where you go, there was someone out there who was crooked and more. Once he was done having his way, he made me fix myself; as he began leaving out.

I laid there crying my eyes out and I prayed Bailey did not get what just happened to me. Trust me it was not a good feeling at all, and I would not wish this on my worst enemy. The moment I was thinking about giving Clever my love, I get raped again. I wanted to know why this kept happening to me, so I got on my knees and prayed to the man upstairs. After I was done, I stayed up all night, I could not sleep at all and I was worried about Bailey.

The next day the guard came and got me, he looked at me and asked if it was ok. I had to lie to him because most of all I feared what the hell could happen to me here. I was no bitch, but this guard clearly had the upper hand on me, and I would not dare test it. I learned my lesson long ago. I made it to the eating area to see Bailey facing the window and she looked really scared. I walked up to her and she jumped out in fear, she hugged me tight and I knew the same thing happened to her last night.

I needed Aaron and Clever to get us out of here fast, this girl walked up on us and asked to speak with us. She mentioned she owns part of the place and she was here to help, the only thing was I did not trust anyone. She told us how her brother Sam mentioned for her to do him a big favor, when she mentioned Faheem's name she blushed, and I could tell she liked him. She rubbed her hand against the bruises on my face and Bailey arm, she asked us what happened but there was no way we were saying anything. I just wanted to be out of this place fast as hell, I could kill them bitches for getting me in this damn place.

There was no way we were going to be able to make up an excuse for these bruises. Clever knew when my ass was lying and Aaron knew when we were lying, so I was shit out of luck. The truth would soon have to come out and that guard's life would be on the line if we were not in this place and he didn't have that uniform on. I would have killed him myself. Sani kept talking and we listened carefully to her, she got our bail, and the money was put up for us through the bail bonds. Most likely we get released Monday morning after seeing the judge, I hated spending another night in his bitch.

Faheem

When Sam came back with the info from his sister, my stomach turned. How the fuck did they get bruises in jail, like where the hell was the guard at. I knew for sure that they were not letting a bitch bully them, something was not right and none of this shit sat well with me. Clever and Aaron going to fucking flip when they find out this shit, they needed to be out of there fast. I am not trusting shit right now and I could not shake the feeling that something was up.

I dapped Sam up and headed out, he said to himself that something did not seem right. Plus, they did not want to tell her what happened, they were saving someone's ass and I couldn't understand why. I pulled up to Junior school and saw Tina ass trying to get him, she looked a mess and ruff like she had a long night. Junior was in daycare and he sometimes went there on Saturday for play dates with the other kids.

I parked and got out making my way to them, she was really making a big scene out here. All the parents stopped looking at her and some were even taking pictures of her. Junior saw me and ran over to me, I picked him up and he held me tight. The teacher began telling me what happened, and I couldn't believe this bitch tried to sneak him out of the school. I thanked the teacher and began walking away from the crowd with Junior still in my arms, he was crying and clearly scared.

"Give me my baby Faheem" she shouted at me

"He doesn't want to go with you, so stop making a scene and go clean yourself up" I said shaking my head

"You will pay for this" she shouted one last time

Some dude in an all-white Benz pulled up and she got in, how did this nigga allow his girl to be looking all bummed. Tina had her priorities fucked up and I was not going to let her drag my son down with her. I jumped in my truck and we headed out, I talked to him for a while and it made me smile.

"Hey little man what's up" I asked him

"Hey dad" he said smiling

"Where you want to go" I asked him

"Uncle house" he said laughing

I already knew he wanted to see the babies and his uncles, he seemed so happy around us. He asked me about Abbey and Bailey, and I could not really find the right words to tell him. We pulled up to Aaron house and saw them sitting outside smoking, I parked, and we got out. He ran off giving them handshakes before going inside to find the babies, Momma Alice was in there, so I knew they were safe. I might as well move on this damn street because my ass is always over here, I should have listened to Aaron when he preached a lot of shit to me.

I dapped them up and took a seat, Clever passed me the blunt and I began telling the news I found out. They were just as mad, and we just could not understand what the hell was going on in there. They have not been calling since the last time and we just knew they would call every change they got. I called my lawyer, and he will be representing them in court. He was good at his job and I knew he could get them out of anything. We put the money up for them already through the bail bonds, all we had to do now was wait and we really could not wait any longer.

Theses couple of days seemed like they been gone months, I am not used to coming here and not seeing Abbey talking shit to me or Bailey mugging my head. I really missed my sisters a lot and that was no place for them, Abbey grew a temper after her father raped her. She was only able to tolerate so much before she snapped out, I knew for sure she got into a fight. Momma Alice came out passing us all something she just made, the shit was good as hell and I see where Abbey get it from.

"All the kids are cleaned up and sleep" Momma Alice said

"How do you do it ma?" Aaron asked

"I got the magic touch" she laughed

"I miss my babies though, did yall find out when they come home" she said a little upset

"Yeah ma Monday" I said hugging her

We sat outside and talked for a while, I would just finish my classes at a community college or online. I was going to become a pro ball player and there was not shit a bitch can do to stop me. My son needed me more than anything now and I was not going to let him down, he will grow up to know that I am that nigga who will always have his back. We chilled on the front porch and everyone was just sitting here quietly looking at the sky. God had the answer to all our prayers, and we were ready to do the right thing.

My phone began vibrating in my pocket and I pulled it out, everyone else pulled out their phones also and I wondered did we all get a text from Aden. I thought my brother was dead and here he goes sending us messages. I wondered what the hell he wanted, he really stabbed us all in the back.

"I know none of yall fuck with the kid but I'm man enough to admit that I've fucked up bad. I am not mad that y'all will not forgive me because if it were the other way around it would be hard for me too. Look all I am saying is I am sorry, and I know I cut deep but my forgiveness is pure. I am going to church now and I have been baptized with my wife Shelly. Love yall Fam" Aaron read Aden text out loud

Everyone sat there quiet and had no words, I did not plan on accepting his apology just yet. I mean he is my brother and I love him, but he really fucked up bad. Aaron just sat there and the look on his face was wired, it looked like he was having mixed emotions right now. I understood though because all Aaron ever wanted for us was to be better and stay out the streets. Aden was just like our father, the streets were their home, and they loved it.

Aaron and I on the other hand did not look at it like that, our family came before the streets and we wanted to follow the dreams we had. The streets were never my home but when my father needed me, I was there. Aaron left his career in Atlanta to come back and help my father, when our father got locked up Aden really got out of hand. Pushing him to the back of my head I looked up to see Tina and Rena walking our way. These bitches were pushing it and I was not a woman beater, but I will fuck one of these hoes up. They stood there looking at us and I could see the bruises on them clearly. Rena had a black eye, and her nose was broken plus she had a cast on her arm, Tina had a broken arm, and both their faces was fucked up. I laughed out loud because my sisters really beat that ass, Rena stood there licking her lips at Clever and he got ticked off.

"Bitch if you don't get from by my brother house" he said mad as hell

"Baby why are you being like that?" Rena said smiling

"Bitch my baby locked up because of you" he said standing up

"That bitch can't do for you like I can" she said again

"Yeah my wife can do more for me, what you did was reckless" he spazzed out

He was close enough to choke her ass and everything she said about Abbey ticked him off more. He really loved Abbey and he would not give her up for anything trust me I saw it with my own eyes. He raised his hand pulling it back, he was about to smack the spit out her mouth until Momma Alice grabbed his hand.

"Son, it's not worth it, your daughter needs you and most of all Abbey needs you" she said calming him down

"Daddy baby crying" junior came running out

"Mommy baby" Tina smiled

He began backing up and Clever took him back inside, he was so scared of going with his mom it was crazy. I wanted to know what really takes place at her house, there was another reason besides him getting hit. Momma Alice stepped in and made them leave, they screamed it wasn't over, but I think it is. Abbey had no fear in pulling a trigger since her father raped her, these girls better sit down if they love life. When Abbey swung Bailey followed up, they became savages and there was only so much we could do. They were scared for life from what they fathers and Aden did, they really fucked up their lives in many ways. I went into the house to check on my bro, he was really going though it with Abbey gone and I understood because she was the heart of this family. She kept everyone together and without her I can see shit will never be the same.

Chapter 18
Abbey

I honestly could not wait to get the fuck out of here, that guard touched me every night since I been here. I have been trying to keep my composure but if I am here any longer, I will do something to hurt him. I had more bruises than before and this was getting out of hand, not to mention I had to deal with this dyke bitch. This bitch looked just like a man, she always trying to bully me, but I fucked her up plenty of times. I know a lot because dealing with my father taught me a lot, these cops are crooked as hell and I planned to change my major from medical to law. I wanted to take down every crooked ass cop, I got the urge to throw up and that is exactly what happened. Sharp pain went through my stomach and I grabbed it feeling a lot of pain, I could not move as they screamed for head count. The guard Jimmy came in and smiled at me, the words that left his mouth made me wish I could kill him.

"Oh, look who is in pain, you better get your ass up and oh I will be seeing you tonight" he smiled walking out.

I could not take this shit no more tomorrow could not come fast enough, I did not feel right, and something was really making me sick. After they did the count Bailey and I went to sit at a table and we talked, I told her everything that just happened to me and the answer she gave I was not expecting. There was no way I could be pregnant by that prick, Clever will kill his ass and probably be mad at me too. I could not stop him from raping me and I damn sure could not tell anyone, I was fucked. These bitches come and sit at our table, we roll our eyes and continue talking. These bitches were a little bigger than us and their hair was nappy as hell like they never comb the shit. She gets up and pulls my hair and I snapped out. This bitch was always bothering me. Like I do not know if she gay or not, but I do not roll that way. I got up and she swung at me but missed, throwing a three piece I hit her in the nose.

She stumbled back and her friend tried to jump on me, but Bailey got on her quick, we got put in the hole and I hated it. The night slowly approaches, and I get scared as I hear the keys jiggling. Jimmy soon came to the door and unlocked it, I stood up backing into the wall wishing there was somewhere to go. He walked up on me and pulled down my pants, he rammed himself inside of me. He began putting one of his hands around my neck and I started losing breath, he started talking crazy and I want this to be over already.

"I had some of your friends over there, but she wasn't as good as you" he smiled down at me.

I began moving around trying to get loose and he smacked me, I fell to the ground and blood was licking from my mouth. He bent down to my level and promised me he would see me on the streets. My heart rate sped up and once again I will be looking over my shoulder, this shit was getting out of hand. Little did he know he would get himself hurt. I will kill his ass on the streets if Clever does not first.

I laid there on the ground in pain, I could not move and did not plan to. My body was so sore that it felt like I was chained up to the bed again. Looking at Jimmy I saw my father, they were so much alike that it made my blood boil. The morning slowly approaches, and this new guard comes to get me. He looked at me weird and I began to wonder, do he see what I see? He began asking me questions and I was not sure how to answer them. Most of all I was afraid he would not be able to help me at all.

"Hey Abbey!!! Are you ok?" He asked, staring at me.

"Ummm I'm fine" I said without looking at him.

"You don't seem like it, but I'll let it slide for now" he said, not taking his eye off me.

"Officer Johnson, I'm scared" I said looking around.

Before he could say anything else, Jimmy walked up on us and he stood there. My body got tense and my heart rate sped up, officer Johnson noticed how my mood changed. He walked me back to my cell, while Jimmy stared at me the whole time and my hands began to sweat. He asked me questions about Jimmy and I just stayed quiet.

Jimmy

My boy Chris and I were out in the parking lot having lunch, we chilled and talked for a while. I missed my boy and I am glad his ass came back, he didn't know what I was doing to inmates. Since I had a piece of Abbey ass, I needed to brag about it and tell him how good shorty is. He sat at the table looking at his phone and I began talking seeing what he was up to.

"How's your son doing?" I asked him.

"He's good," he said in one breath.

"So, let me tell you how I had some of the sweetest pussy," I said, smiling hard as hell.

"Oh word" he said looking up at me.

"Yeah man!!! She is an inmate and her name is Abbey" I said licking my lips.

"What the hell Jimmy?" he said standing up.

"Look bro chill damn, it's other guards out here" I said standing up, but Chris was already walking away.

I went looking for Chris to try and explain my point, but they said his ass left for the rest of today. I got pissed as hell and hoped he did not open his mouth. I walked around the prison looking in the cells, I noticed Abbey was gone and got even madder. I was going to find her on the street, and she will be seeing me again real soon.

Clever

I wanted to know how my baby was holding up in there, this shit was becoming beyond stressful. Rena ass better stay away from my house before something happens to her. She made me hate her so much more now, she was always running around messing up my life. She was not fucking it up this time, I would not dare let her either. I packed Kelsie up and headed out for a while, being in this house without Abbey killing me.

I pulled up to the supermarket and parked, I got out putting the baby holder on. Once I had it tight and secure, I put Kelsie in, and we made our way into the store. We needed more food so when my baby gets home, she will not have to do it, the baby needs milk also. Looking down I noticed her knocked out, I smiled because once she was on my chest she fell right to sleep.

Making my way down the baby aisle someone began screaming my name. Turning around I saw my cousin Chris, we were unbreakable and always had each other's backs. When my parents moved us away it was the worst, I did not have my brother with me. We did everything together and I missed this nigga when I was in Trenton.

"Well if it isn't my brother from another mother" he said pushing a stroller.

"Man, bro I missed your crazy ass," I said, giving him dap.

"For real man!! What has been up? When you get back in town?" He said

"Nothing man trying to get my future wife Abbey out of that damn jail, while holding everything down at home" I said honestly

"I work at a jail and I know half the inmates there, I know her well I've met her" he said honestly

"Does she really have bruises?" I asked him concerned

"Yeah bro she does and there's this guard that's been touching her" he said disgusted.

"What do you mean Chris?" I said uneasy

"He been raping her" he said again

"Ima kill him" I said mad as hell.

"Look we could set him up bro, you know I got you bro" he said again

We exchanged numbers and went our separate ways, I could not believe my baby was going through that again. My phone began ringing and I looked at the time, noticing I was running late for court, I turned around and left right away. I made it to the courthouse just in time, momma Alice stood outside waiting. I parked and got out grabbing baby girl. She took Kelsie from me and told me to hurry up and go in.

I did as was told and headed for the courtroom, I walked in taking my seat next to Aaron and she did not come out yet. They soon brought them both in and they looked rough as hell, I was getting pissed as hell. After spending hours in court, they got off on probation, meaning if they got into any more trouble they would go back to jail. This shit was crazy as hell and I'm glad they are coming home though, I needed to know what the fuck was going on.

We made it home and they hugged one last time before going their separate ways. Aaron and I just looked at each other before following close behind with the kids. I walked in and laid Kelsie in her swing, I headed to the room and I could hear the shower running. I laid on the bed and waited for her to come out, she soon came out and began getting dressed. She laid on the bed with tears in her eyes. I knew what happened, but I wanted her to tell me.

"How are you holding up baby?" I asked her

"Not so good, baby I was raped in there" she said crying now

"I know my cousin Chris told me, I promise I'm going to kill that nigga" I said wiping her tears

"Officer Johnson?" She questioned

"Yes baby" I laughed a little

We laid there talking and She told me everything that happened, I was not letting my baby go back to that place for nothing. All I ever wanted was to make her happy, I never wanted any of this for her. She *deserves so much better and I wanted to be the one who gave her that.*

Chapter 19
Abbey

It felt so good to be home with my family, damn I missed them so much. My mind kept drifting to how Clever already knew what happened, now that I think about it, Chris and Clever did favor each other. Kelsie began crying and I got up following her sound. I picked her up and she got quiet, I rocked her, and she smiled at me. She slowly drifted back to sleep and I laid her down in the swing turning it on. I sat on the sofa and began looking through my phone. I've missed a lot of crazy shit since I've been gone. I was glad my family had nothing to do with it though, the knock on the door broke my thoughts quickly. Clever was gone taking a test and it was just Kelsie and I here. Looking through the peephole I saw Faheem and junior, I let them in, and we headed to take a seat.

Junior was happy with his dad that it amazed me so much, and Faheem was an incredibly good father to him. We sat and talked about everything, Faheem was really stressed out. That damn baby mom of his was really trying to fuck up my boy life. I told him he better not let the shit happen, because he was way smarter than that. I didn't want to see him make the same mistake I made, there was another knock on the door and I got pissed off.

I got up to see who the hell it could be this time, I looked out the peephole to see Faheem baby Mom standing there. Why was this hoe knocking on my door, I quickly opened the door and the shocked look on her face made me laugh.

"How can I help you?" I asked her with a smile

"Where is Faheem" she asked not looking at me

"He is in there chilling, why?" I asked again

"Could you tell him I'm here for junior" she said looking up

"Faheem" I yelled for him

He soon walked up and he was pissed as hell when he saw her face. It was like he hated seeing the sight of her and she stood there speechless as hell. She looked from me to Faheem and I guess she thought I was about to walk away. Naw she had me fucked up this my house for one and for two I don't trust the bitch.

"What do you want?" He hissed at her

"My son!! I want to take him somewhere Faheem please" she said scared as hell

"Hell no!!! You know the dam rules, plus he don't want to go with you after that stunt you pulled at the school" he said in a deep tone

"Let's ask him" she said mad

He called for junior and he came running to the sound of his dad's voice. Once he reached us his whole facial expression changed, he seemed upset she was here. I wondered what the hell went on why I was away, this bitch had to do some crazy shit for her own kid to blow her off. He just stood there behind Faheem leg quiet as a mouse, she talked to him and he ignored her.

I began walking away because she was making me mad, someone grabbed my hand and I looked down to see junior. He walked with me into the kitchen and he sat down at the table. I pulled out some cookies and milk, I sat at the table with cups and opened the cookies. We ate cookies and he began looking around, you could hear his parents arguing at the front door. I tried to do different things to keep him in mind but I just couldn't.

He looked at me with his eyes filled with tears, I got up going around the table to sit next to him. He laid on my chest and began crying, I felt his pain and I understood how it felt not to be loved by one of your parents. He began talking and I felt bad because the little man was so heartbroken. I Held him tight as he continued to talk to me.

"Auntie I love my mom but I'll rather live with my daddy" he said low

"Why what's wrong" I asked concerned

"She don't love me like daddy loves me" he said again

"Your only 2 in half years old, how do you know" I questioned him

"Daddy shows it and mommy don't, I'm smart auntie I know" he said laughing

I laughed at him and he began telling me about school, this little boy was way too smart and I guess that saying is true. Kids know when they are loved or not, however that shit goes I laughed out loud. Faheem soon joined us and we all sat and ate cookies while junior told us stories about school. The little boy was a comedian and I loved his little soul to death, Kalsie began crying and Junior ran off to her before I even got to move. Faheem and I busted out laughing following behind him.

Clever

Once I finished my test I turned it in and headed out, I needed to get back home to my babies. Them begin there alone didn't sit right with me, I prayed Faheem made it over there to check on them. I made it outside heading straight for my car, once I reached it I saw these bitches sitting on my shit. This bitch was really trying me , and momma Alice wasn't here to stop me from slapping the spit out her mouth.

She smiled at me and it made me sick to my stomach, there was no way I would take the bitch back. She was the type of bitch to mess up a happy home, if she messed this one up she will get fucked up. About to spaz out she began walking towards me with this little ass green shirt, the bitch looked a mess if you asked me.

These boys came out and stood around me, now I was really pissed off. They some real bitch niggas trying to jump me, but I will get each one of them back with my crew. I took boxing as a kid so I could take at least two of them, he swung and I hit him with a three piece. The others charged at me and I fought my way out of this shit, I heard my name beng called and I knew the voice right away.

Aaron, Faheem and I stood in a circle while being surrounded by at least 6 niggas. We looked at each other and got ready for the fight ahead of us, Rena began talking and her voice was annoying as hell. I don't know why she thinks this was going to make me come running back. I was no bitch nigga and neither was Aaron or Faheem, this crew clearly had us fucked up and they was all over the place.

They came running up on us swinging and we did what we are known for, I didn't come here to get back into bad shit and that's exactly what Rena wanted. She was going to get herself hurt real bad, she began walking towards me and I wanted to choke her ass.

"Now you either drop the hoe and come back to the gang or they will hurt you tonight" she said smiling

"Bitch please" I said smiling back at her

"I told my brothers Jimmy and Mark about this and they isn't happy at all" she said walking away

My blood started to boil, first off I didn't even know the bitch had a brother. I wondered if it was the same Jimmy who harmed Abbey, she jumped in a car after snapping her fingers. The six guys came at us again and something had to be done, it was now my time to send a message.

One of them stabbed me in the shoulder and I yelled in pain, pulling it out I chopped him in the throat making him fall to the ground. Everyone was now down and he was the last man standing, I needed him to give a message for me. Rena knew me better than that and I don't know why she thinks I'm weak, but she will stop trying me.

"Tell Rena she better stay far away from me and my family, or else she will be taking her last breath. Let them know Clever is back in town" I said pushing him to the ground

He got up and ran off fast as hell, they helped me to the truck and we got in heading home. Faheem called the doctor on the way, so he will meet us there. Abbey ass is going to freak the fuck out, when I felt a little better I had to text Chris and tell him get the old crew back together. Let them know I'm back in town, now everyone here knows not to mess with me because of who my father was.

Bailey

The boys have yet to come back, Aaron and Faheem left hours ago to check on Clever. No one was answering their phone, there was a knock on the door and I got up to get it since Abbey was zoned out. She cared about Clever a lot and I never saw her like this over no one. I opened the door to see Chris standing there, he came in asking for Clever and we had no answer.

The door flew open and the boys walked in, Clever was bleeding while Faheem and Aaron held him up. Abbey began freaking out and I took her to my house to calm down a little, once we got inside the house she broke down crying. I could see the pain in her eyes and I felt that same hurt she was feeling. I knew that bitch Rena had something to do with this, I had no clue why they were trying us but I was ready to turn out. Fuck what the judge had to say, but for my twins I had to do the right thing.

Aaron soon came home. He was a bloody mess, that had to be a deep ass cut. I wonder what the hell happened, this shit was getting out of hand. Aaron sat on the sofa across from us, and began telling us everything. Abbey got so heated she grabbed my keys and ran out, I prayed she didn't do anything crazy. Aaron hit the wall and it made a hole, he was pissed and I knew he only wanted to make things better for us.

"Shit!!! She better be ok" he said grabbing his keys and walking out

He called for Faheem and I watched them jump in the truck speeding off. Clever's car was still at the school so I hope they find her there. I went back to Clever and Abbey house to check on the kids, I walked in to see Clever sitting on the coach zoned out. When he saw me he jumped up like I was Abbey, but how would I tell him she left my house at full speed. Clever looked at me and he knew something was wrong, Abbey always had a hard life and this right here was too much.

Chapter 20
Clever

When Bailey told me that Abbey left in a hurry furious, I knew for sure it couldn't be good and I didn't want to see her get locked back up. I got up in a hurry not paying any of the pain no mind, I needed to find my baby ASAP and I hope Aaron and Faheem find her before anything. Chris followed close behind me and said he will drive, we pulled up to the college and I saw my windows busted out. Rena ass was taking it too far and now a bitch was going to pay me for my car.

My phone began ringing off the hook. Before I could say hello I heard all this screaming. Faheem caught her hurry up, Aaron screamed before he came back to the phone. He was all out of breath and I told him to catch it before he started talking. I wonder who the hell they are trying to catch, even though Abbey was big boned her ass can run fast as hell.

"Yo bro where are you at?" H asked in a hurr

"In the car looking for Abbey ass" I said mad and upset

"We found her chasing Rena ass down the street, Rena busted your windows out" he said irritated

"Where y'all at" I said in a hurry

"Around the Corner from the college, by this dam field" he said before yelling at Faheem again

"On my way" I said ending the call

We go around the Corner and I can see Abbey chasing Rena, the bitch was scared as hell. Faheem finally caught her and she started going off. I got out trying to calm her down. She told me what Rena did besides busting my windows out and I got pissed off. I looked down at her and there was this bruise on her arm.

Rena stopped running when these dudes showed up and we stood around Abbey, Abbey's eyes got big and I knew for sure he was the Jimmy I was looking for. The other dude looked very familiar, he was the dude from jersey. Now the bitch wanted to act tough cause her brothers were here, a bitch wasn't going to touch Abbey not why I'm here anyways.

"Oh bitch don't get scared now" Rena laughed

"Says the one who ran to her brothers for help" Abbey mocked her laugh

"Bitch watch it" Rena said pissed

"No boo I'm just getting started!!! The difference between us is I don't need them but I know they are always there anyway. You on the other hand talk mad shit but can't back it up always ready to running to your brothers" Abbey laughed harder

"I told you I will see you on the street" Jimmy said

"Now I'm telling you that you will get hurt and you better keep little sis in your pocket because I will see her on the street again" Abbey said one more time

"Where's my daughter" the other one said

"What daughter bitch!!! As I remember you don't have one and our daughter very good" Abbey said walking away

They tried to run up on her and I wasn't having that shit, all three of them got shot fucked up. Dude never even wanted Kalsie, now he wants to scream where my daughter. That nigga has no rights to her and Farrah made sure of that, Abbey was pissed as hell when we reached Chris truck. The look on her face told me that she was mad as hell, Farrah left all rights of Kalsie to Abbey and she hated seeing that nigga face he killed her best friend.

"Chris, did you make that call?" I asked him

"Yeah I did and everyone was happy as hell your back" he said shaking his head laughing

"I'm that nigga, that's why" I said joking around

"They asked about your girl and daughter though" he said in code

"You know the shit already and as you can see she needs it or her ass will be back in jail" I said again

"I see you finally met your match" he laughed harder

"Bay did you hear that nigga, screaming his daughter? I swear if he comes anywhere near her I will kill him myself" She butted in

"Bay don't let it get to you" I said trying to calm her down

"Naw I'm not trying to hear none of that, I'm tired of running and I'm tired of people thinking they can run over me" she hissed at me

"She worse than you; we can say, the gang going to be scared of her ass" Chris added In laughing at me

She sat in the back seat quiet as a mouse and I knew for sure if I went back to the gang my baby got me 100% but this not what I really wanted. I had to protect my family though and Abbey ass needed all the help she can get. Her ass would have ended up back in jail because the bitch a snitch, my boys will keep her protected and do the dirty work with her if not for her.

We pulled up to the house and she jumped out heading straight in the house, I sat and talked with Chris for a while. My baby was really mad and I understood why, it was almost like no matter what trouble followed her. We came here for a new start but yet all we get is trouble, he dapped me up and I got out heading inside. Abbey laid on the sofa with Kalsie on her chest and Bailey was rubbing her hair, my baby was hurting badly.

I walked into the kitchen to get something to drink, my side began hurting. I was moving around way too much, breaking my thoughts. I can hear their convo and Abbey was hurt badly. She cried and I couldn't take it any more, I walked out the kitchen and Bailey stood up. Bailey left us alone and Abbey laid on my chest crying, she told me how she was feeling and I had no clue she felt that way.

Abbey

It started to seem like no matter where we went trouble followed us, I couldn't believe Mark and Jimmy were Rena brothers. They were playing the game wrong on the streets and I could show them how to play real good. That nigga never cared about Kalsie at all, he tried to kill Farrah while still pregnant after he found out. That family was nuts and I subjected them to leave me alone, my dad did bad things to me along with other people.

I grew a short temper from everything and I don't tolerate the bullshit, Chris was right when he said Clever met his match because I was a reflection of him. I laid on his chest watching a baby girl in the swing, I just wanted to be left alone and be happy. I couldn't escape it if I tried and just like I promised I would see her again and very soon. Clever was having a little get together here tomorrow and I couldn't wait to meet his family and friends. I'm pretty sure Chris mentioned how crazy I am to them already, now Jimmy was playing my game.

I was so deep in thought that I fell asleep, a couple hours later Kalsie began crying and I knew my baby was hungry and wet. I got up to see Clever knocked out, I quickly grabbed her calming her down so she wouldn't wake daddy. Going into the kitchen I made her and the twins a bottle warming them up because they will be awake soon. I rocked her back and forth while talking about Farrah. I did this from time to time because I wanted her to know who was in some way. I knew Farrah was watching over us.

Checking the bottle it was just right, going to the room I laid her on the bed and grabbed everything to change her. Making it back to the bed she began crying again, I picked her up and began feeding her. She drank half the bottle of milk and was knocked out again. Burping her I then laid her down to change her pamper. The twin, ma, and I were also here so once I got her settled I needed to get them because they are now crying, good thing I warmed the bottles up already. I put Kalsie in the middle of the bed before going to get the twin, once I reached them I picked each one up at time rocking them.

I reached my room and did the same thing I've done with Kalsie, Drew went to sleep first and Dakota fought the crap out of her sleep. Once she finally got to sleep I put pillows around the other side, I laid by Kalsie and drifted back to sleep. My mind wandered in every direction before I was all the way out. I woke up to Clever staring at me, he looked at me crazy and it made me look at the time. It was damn near 4:30pm and I still had the twins. I got up stretching before going into the bathroom.

Once I took my 30 minute shower and brushed my teeth, I walked back into the room to see everyone gone. I got dressed in my all black jumpsuit, I walked out the room to see Clever making the babies laugh. They were now 6 months old and time was flying, with all the drama going on around us I prayed these babies stayed safe.